EMPE~~~

Colin Thubron is the author of several classic master-
pieces of travel writing, including *Among the Russians*,
Behind the Wall, *The Lost Heart of Asia* and *In Siberia*.
His fiction titles include *A Cruel Madness* (winner of the
1985 Silver Pen Award), *Falling* and *Distance*.

ALSO BY COLIN THUBRON

Colin Thubron

EMPEROR

VINTAGE

Published by Vintage 2002

2 4 6 8 10 9 7 5 3 1

First published in Great Britain by
William Heinemann 1978

Vintage
Random House, 20 Vauxhall Bridge Road,
London SW1V 2SA

Random House Australia (Pty) Limited
20 Alfred Street, Milsons Point, Sydney
New South Wales 2061, Australia

Random House New Zealand Limited
18 Poland Road, Glenfield,
Auckland 10, New Zealand

Random House (Pty) Limited
Endulini, 5A Jubilee Road, Parktown 2193,
South Africa

The Random House Group Limited Reg. No. 954009
www.randomhouse.co.uk

A CIP catalogue record for this book
is available from the British Library

ISBN 0 099 28729 3

The Random House Group Limited supports The Forest Stewardship
Council (FSC®), the leading international forest certification organisation.
Our books carrying the FSC label are printed on FSC® certified paper.
FSC is the only forest certification scheme endorsed by the leading
environmental organisations, including Greenpeace. Our
paper procurement policy can be found at
www.randomhouse.co.uk/environment

MIX
Paper from
responsible sources
FSC
www.fsc.org   FSC® C018072

Printed and bound in Great Britain by Clays Ltd, St Ives PLC

For Monica Mason

The conversion to Christianity of the Emperor Constantine is a watershed in Western history. But this book is not a historical inquiry. Of Constantine too little is known to ascertain so ambiguous a character as I have indicated. Of the Empress Fausta almost nothing is known at all.

Rather I have attempted to explore regions on which history is silent. I have been anxious only not to trespass beyond the bounds of the possible.

Colin Thubron

Melitius, lately Master of Studies to the Augustus Constantine. To Celsus, professor of rhetoric.

Constantinople, 30 May [A.D. 338]

I AM sending you these papers by my personal messenger. You will understand why, after you have read them. What I have to tell you is in strictest secrecy.

A year ago I dined with the Augustus Constantine and several of his close ministers. It was not a formal evening, but the kind of relaxation in which he indulged towards the end of his life. I think the wine must have emboldened me, but since Constantine had several times patted my shoulder almost affectionately, I dared to mention the vision which had converted him to Christianity more than quarter of a century ago. My father, I said, had been present.

I must have been mad to mention it. The expression on His Eternity's face changed dramatically. You remember how he could stare at one, tautening his lips? He must also have turned whiter, because the rouge on his cheeks was suddenly very obvious. He said angrily: "The matter has been recorded by the Sacred Historian."

As you may imagine, I did not know where to look. I stammered an apology. But later I noticed that the Augustus was frowning to himself and kept shifting his position on the couch. Suddenly he leant towards me again, and with an odd perplexity in those intemperate eyes he asked: "What did your father say occurred?"

Yes, *he* was asking *me* what had happened!

I replied: "My father never spoke of it, Eternity." (This was true; at the mention of Constantine's vision my father was always silent.)

The Augustus checked himself at once, as if remembering who I was (or who he was). He never alluded to the matter again.

It occurred to me then how we learn to evade our past if it is not creditable to us, and to believe our own lies. As for an emperor, the truth is contorted before his eyes. He is surrounded by men who will banish his every mistake into an oblivion of flattery.

Is this what happened to Constantine? I don't know. It only seems to me that for 25 years the Church has been evolving more and more extravagant accounts of his conversion, and that already these are becoming the official truth.

This was the last time I spoke to the Emperor. A month later he was dead.

It was then, while I was still Master of Studies, that I started my investigations. My father Synesius, as you know, was the Emperor's private secretary throughout the early years, and after his death I found the cubicula of his house on the Quirinal filled with papers locked in chests. These included the Augustus' journal, kept over the months of his invasion of Italy, much of it written in his own hand. I also took advantage of my custodianship of the Imperial Archives to copy down those documents relevant to the period. I transcribed letters gathered by the secret police after the execution of the Empress Fausta; even the letters of her lady companion, a certain Livilla Politta; together with copies of correspondence from the Bishop of Cordoba. (Oh yes, the secret police then were quite as efficient as they are now.)

The result of my findings has not the clarity of state propaganda. But it has, I think, the complexity of truth.

Do you think that posterity would condemn me for bringing these things to the light? Or is the truth better lost for ever? Should we be blind and happy, or honest and disillusioned? An old debate.

I cannot send you everything I have. But I've copied the documents most relevant to that least explicable happening of our era: the conquest of a Roman emperor by a Galilean prophet. That period seems now as remote as Romulus, I know. But it made us what we are – a Christian Empire – and will shape the world to come for as long as any of us can predict.

I enjoin on you again the need for secrecy. I await your advice.

Celsus to Melitius.

Constantinople, 2 June

I WILL not read them. We live in a Christian world now, whatever you or I may feel. What do you think to gain by these disclosures? To spread the truth by gossip? If I did not know you better, I would think you had lost your senses.

You are right when you indicate that the present shapes the past. Now it is not only shaped, but fleshed and firm and credible. It cannot be changed; and I am too old to try, and to die for nothing.

So I return the papers to you, their seals unbroken, and with this advice: Forget.

THE PAPERS

In A.D. 306 Gaius Flavius Constantine, the son of an uneducated but talented Illyrian soldier, succeeded his father as Augustus of Britain and Gaul by the acclamation of his legions in York. During the next few years the Roman Empire was split by civil war, and in the summer of 312 Constantine marched over the Alps against his rival Maxentius in Rome, and laid siege to Verona. He was still a pagan. And he had been married five years to Maxentius' own sister, Fausta.

PART ONE

✻

VERONA

I

Before Verona, 23 August A.D. 312

NINTH report of this month from Rome:
   Population continues restless. On 7 August, after thefts by
Sicilian troops, there was a three-hour riot among shopkeepers
near Trajan's Forum; they openly vilified the tyrant Maxentius.

There are rumours of another senator's estate confiscated, and
of his daughters given to army officers. Senators are starting to
withhold gifts to the tyrant, in the evident hope that his days
are few.

Ill omens increase. It is said that on the Capitoline Hill the
statues of the gods are sweating blood. A cat by the Temple of
Uranus was heard to speak. Many people attest this.

August 8: two thousand Moorish light cavalry landed in Ostia
as reinforcements to Carthaginian auxiliaries; horses very sick,
some dead.

May the Augustus live for ever.

II

*From the Commonplace Book of Synesius, Master
of the Sacred Memory and private secretary to
Constantine.*

[The diary of the pagan Secretary is incomplete. He appears to have written it
for some posterity, but later, because of the unfavourable times, to have
suppressed it.]

I WOULD not have believed, a year ago, that I could survive among the siege-works of an army. Yet now I sit at a table in a broken apartment house not two stadia from the walls of Verona, and does this old hand shake? No. Curious what tricks life plays on us. As a young man, when I was quite muscular, I spent my time gossiping like a woman in the corridors of the Sacred Consistory. Now, when I am – as my grandchildren tell me – all dried up like a dead spider, I find myself campaigning in the field.

Last night, while I watched the fording of the Adige river, I even felt a pang of – dare I say it? – youthful excitement. This disgusts me. It's thirty years since anything, even a woman, turned these withered senses to fire. And now I find myself excited by what? – a few thousand men with torches wading across a river to kill people on the other side. When Constantine noticed me among his staff he asked: "Do you want to cross over, Secretary?"

I suppose I turned pale, poor old Synesius.

"Your interests exclude military tactics?" he continued, "or are you reluctant to die for science, as Pliny did?" After that he passed across with his commanders, leaving me on the safer side. I did not know he had even heard of Pliny. I waited by the river with the rest of the secretariat – a pitiful bunch we were in the wet dawn – watching the baggage wagons cross over and Frankish auxiliaries staking out earthworks to defend the ford. After a while the bodies of men and horses began floating past us, and we went back to the main lines.

Sometimes I feel it is best to experience as little as possible. I have become so accustomed to the sight of blood that this afternoon I witnessed the execution of two soldiers for cowardice. All that occurred to me was that their severed heads went rolling about just like dice. This only goes to show what I have always held: that horrors do not sharpen but blunt the senses. An old friend once set above his vestibule door the blood-soaked cuirass in which his father was killed. He put it there, he said, as a perpetual reminder of the horror of violence. And was he reminded? The first time he passed the vestibule, yes. The second time, maybe. The third time not at all, and thereafter he grew used to it, and was later killed in an amphitheatre riot with his fingers on another man's throat.

As for myself, in a single month I seem to have experienced all the miseries of soldiering. I've been frozen in the Cottian Alps, bored at Milan, terrified at the Battle of Brescia. And now the mosquitoes of the Po valley are marching against us and are mangling me in this detestable little room.

All the same, it is good to be still at last, before my thighs are rubbed away by my abominable mule. Here we have a change from army millet and salted pork. Mutton is plentiful, and the quartermaster has brought in Rhaetian wine. A real wine at last! This one tastes like a young wife might. Pleasantly firm, with a sweet, full body (and the only companionship I may expect at my time of life.) But it's not for the men. Off duty they get drunk on a brew of fermented vegetables, and these last days the officers have kept a strict watch.

Walking behind the lines this evening, I saw the soldiers sitting between the earth ramparts and their tents. Some of them were hardening the tips of stakes in the camp-fire flames. Others were singing; while the Germans, of course, gambled. Such lean, harsh giants, these Gaulish and German legionaries! It disturbs me to look at them. Barely one among them has known the soft shores of our Mediterranean. Their heads are covered in manes of brown or yellow hair, which the weight of their helmets has compressed into moist sheaths. I confess they amaze me. They camp here, a thousand miles from home, and are paid a pittance to attack an emperor they have never seen. They march thirty miles a day and are forbidden to plunder. Yet for every obscene song about the Augustus there are ten in praise of him.

What touches the heart of such men? They are inured to every pain, their own and others'. They are quarrelsome and ruddy-faced, their lips thin and their eyes blue like a cold sky. The wind does not burnish them, as it does our southern men, but nibbles away the pores to leave great pitted cheeks and the expressions of starved wolves. Their gods are numberless and confused. So far away from home, I think, they lose their hold. The men worship what they can remember in a fierce doggerel before battle; or take to Mithras or Jupiter.

How much they know or understand of anything is impossible to say. But listening to their army Latin, which is half nonsense to me, it seems they regard Italy as a kind of paradise. I don't suppose it occurs to any of them what will happen if we are defeated here. It is said that with this force – only forty thousand, with eight thousand horse – we are outnumbered by three to one. Yet whenever I look at these arrogant men, veterans of the Rhine, I can imagine no army to face them.

All along our lines the enemy walls are easily visible, with the tops of temples and apartment buildings, three or four storeys high, showing above them. Once, in the arcades above a double gate, I saw the silhouettes of archers. The Adige flows wide and greenish in a great curve northwards, cradling the city. I sat among the wagons here and paid a soldier to find me some biscuits. A flock of gulls was moving by the shore. I don't believe in omens, but I watched them. They rose and settled on the river like scraps of linen, and drifted down opposite the enemy walls. Then they lifted all together from the surface, and flew back to us. They did this again and again. It was oddly desolate.

When I returned to our headquarters – if this fetid block can be called that – I saw the Augustus standing alone on the rooftop, unmistakable for his great height, and gazing at the west. He had dismissed his staff for the night, even the evening secretaries. These whims alarm me. More than ever, perhaps, Constantine is decisive and alert. But there is a new truculence about him. I sometimes think he's afraid to be still. Admittedly all his life has been spent moving – on the Rhine, in Syria, Egypt, Persia, fighting or travelling with the court of Diocletian. But ever since he entered Italy, he's changed.

By day his brain is dagger-sharp and he is a furnace of work. He has the whole army, every cohort and outwork, cut into his mind. He foresees everything. At such times people say that the great Sun God is upon him, and I believe that he feels this himself. The legions adore him, but his own staff hold him in fear. The very way he moves creates tension – that rapid, threatening stride. Whatever troubles him – whether an individual or an object – on that he concentrates as if he would drag out its blackest secrets. But the rest of the world he may glance over, not seeing, with a look of abstract superiority. The world flatters him and for that, I think, he despises it. The only person I have never seen him treat like this is his wife Fausta. To her, I notice, he gives his gaze absolutely.

Yet every one of his close retinue has known his kindness. Last February, after one of his orderlies fell into a trembling fit, the

Augustus wrapped him in his own purple cloak. When the orderly recovered he almost died of fright. He thought he would be executed for wearing the purple, and indeed there can be no incident like it in all the annals of our Empire. Because the Augustus is quite like a child. His warmth and generosity are explosive and total, his sense of humour barbarian. One remembers then that he is almost untutored.

But by night something happens. A dark mood comes over him – you can see it approaching like a dream over his face. He dismisses his staff – sometimes all together as tonight. After a light meal he sits me down like a common amanuensis and starts dictating quickly: field orders for the morning, messages to the prefects of the legions or the quartermaster. And all the time, at the end of a day which would have poleaxed other men, he paces the room as if still trying to hold back some immense, unhappy energy. Frequently he clenches his hands at his sides, and has a way of jabbing downwards with his forefinger to enforce a point. He will do this again and again. When the messages are exhausted he sometimes picks a roll of papyrus from a shelf and drops it on the table in front of me. Then he dictates his journal: but only military records. The rest he keeps private, and writes in his own hand. Then, I suspect, it becomes no longer a journal, but a groping inside himself. At this hour I can see that his mind is racing. It is late and he doesn't want me to go. But he will stop and pat my shoulder in his sudden child-like way and say: "But you're tired."

I leave him, I confess, with relief. As I do so I have the impression that I am abandoning him to some black turmoil. My departure is always a betrayal. My bedroom adjoins his chambers, and I hear him tramping back and forth, hour after hour. I had only just got used to the trumpets of the watch, and now this endless noise of his feet keeps me awake, so that yesterday I had the rushes on the floor changed for hay. Sometimes the noise stops and I hear the nervous scraping of an ivory comb on the papyrus, then the scratching of his reed. Some afterthought to the praetorian prefect, perhaps. Or the journal again. What is he saying? I think words to him resemble magic (he is still a peasant at heart). They are a talisman against his own chaos.

But what madness for human beings to inquire into themselves! What can they find? No god, certainly, but a dismembered mess, a kind of colourless nothing.

This evening, yes, I found the Augustus alone on the rooftop watching the sun go down. His father's family worshipped the Sun as the symbol of the Great God; he himself abandoned other gods for this Sun Invincible. He was gazing at it through a ruby, and did not turn round when he heard my footsteps, but pointed to it and said in a half bullying voice: "What is happening there?"

I am far from a religious man. Even my unbelief is not a religion to me. But as a child I was brought up in the credo of Epicurus: fear in man is induced by two fallacies – that the heavenly bodies are divine, and that death is the prelude to pain. Now the Augustus was staring down at me in that quietly formidable way which stops the tongue dead in the mouth. I could find no hint of what way I should answer. So I said: "It is caused, Eternity, by the imposition of the earth in the sun's way. The sun has gone down behind the edge of the earth."

What did he want me to say?

III

Geta, Master of the Offices, to the
Augustus Constantine.

24 August

TENTH report of this month from Rome:
Unconfirmed reports of disaffection among Numidian troops. Details will follow.

It is now common knowledge in the city that more than thirty court sorcerers attend the tyrant – Egyptian and Samaritan for the most part – and that in night-long ceremonies the infernal demons have been invoked against you, my Lord (may the Great God deflect!). Leaden tablets, inscribed with the name of your Eternity and pierced with nails, have been buried under the Palatine Hill.

May the Augustus live for ever.

IV

From the Journal-Memoir of
Constantine Augustus.

THIS morning: inspected the enemy walls again. Impossible to envisage a better defended city. The river wraps it on three sides and is swollen with early rains. Two bridges connect with a fortified hill on the north bank, expensive to assail. All the walls are heavy, and so well bonded that from a distance they look like cliffs.

I search for the point where the enemy thinks himself weak, and a network of ditches is conspicuous before the city's south-western gate. This gate appears older than the ramparts round it, and is half walled up. It is surmounted by a double arcade, at present manned by slingers. I direct the heavy catapults of the Primigenia Legion against it.

To the east the angle of the walls is buttressed by the amphi-theatre, and the defences run too close to the river. Dangerous and constricted for attackers. At midday I crossed the ford and inspected its fortifications. The Frankish auxiliaries have made a poor affair of the far-side camp. I order the engineers of the Ulpia Victrix legion to overhaul. This creates bad feeling. I lose my temper.

Afternoon: consulted with the commanders. We view the enemy hill-citadel, but the approach to it is steep on all sides, and the ascent encumbered by felled trees.

The bulk of our men now on the north bank, and the encircle-ment of the city almost complete. I impress on the commanders the need to menace four or five points at once. Enemy ditches must be systematically filled in. Engineer units of the legions will be responsible for building two mobile towers each.

The generals dislike siege-work and are not used to it. They quarrel and grumble behind my back. The commander of cavalry, Sacrovir, ventures the remark that the enemy general Pompeianus is no more than a perfumed wool-merchant from Milan, and afraid to fight. I laugh at him, something he hates. He will consequently remember what I said: that Pompeianus is the most experienced soldier in Italy.

Now, sitting at this table in an emptied room (and midnight already), I should like to occupy that general's brain. Is he also awake over there? From the upper windows I can see lights, very small and pale, travelling along the ramparts. Our own lines are in darkness except where the Franks still sit about their camp-fires. They gamble for the armour they will strip from the enemy dead: a good sign. Their unmentionable songs float up to these chambers.

It's as well they cannot read. The citizens of Verona have scrawled graffiti on every building outside the walls. Many of these are aimed at me, and the same word appears over and over. 'Matricide.'

I had these erased. I have never seen Rome in my life. So how can I, a Dardanian soldier, look on her as my mother?

Yet strangely it is so. For years now the emperors have abandoned Rome for other cities, but her ghost continues to bestride the world. We have grown on what she gave us; she is our mother and we cannot escape her. But matricide? No! Divinity is no more in Rome than in York. This Matricide is merely a boorish slogan. I am cleansing Rome of a monster, and if her spirit should come to me I'll say: I am your saviour. Twenty years ago in the days of the Emperor Diocletian, the administration of the Empire could be split between several men – and the old magician dominated them all. I myself remember the days when four Augusti and Caesars ruled in brief concord from different capitals. But such edifices can stand only on the prestige of one man. With Diocletian gone, the building fell, and in our time, as in most times, civil war is inevitable. I do not need to ask myself if I am ambitious, because ambition is forced on me. It is the will of the God. Europe is divided between myself and Maxentius, and I must fight until I am alone, or dead.

Even to the secrecy of this journal I can say that this war was not prepared by me, but by him. His statues, as God can see, still stand with honour in the forums of Gaul, while mine were overturned in all his provinces of Italy and Africa. I struck an arm already raised against me. And the people of Rome petitioned me for help, pleading to be saved from a tyranny. If the people are with me, would the gods be against? What gods? Rome is not gods. She is flesh and stones.

I will reverence Rome but not her rulers, who have bled Italy. This is one of the richest provinces of the Empire, but the fields are turning fallow and the irrigation channels falling in. It was Diocletian, I recall, who tied the peasant to his fields by law. It has not worked. The farmers are taxed to their deaths, and sell their children into slavery rather than let them starve. Probably nobody told the old emperor about it. And he thought he was restoring the golden time!

It is an extraordinary fact that a ruler may realise less than his meanest subject. The emperor moves about on vapours of flattery. He knows nobody. Nobody knows him. I spent half my life in the sacred retinue of Diocletian, and addressed him in nothing but formulas. How perfectly I remember that protocol! A step to the right. A bow to the left. Prostration on admittance to the sacred presence, genuflection on leaving it. How was I to know that up on that incense-clouded throne, surrounded by state eunuchs and palatine ministers, the powdered face concealed a man?

Resolution: when I am emperor in Rome I will not powder or rouge my face. I will let people see what I am, even if it is disgusting.

But will I? Already I interpose a false person between myself and my flatterers. This person inspires their fright. Nowadays it takes something sad or weak or humorous to break him down. Then another man emerges, impulsive and rather kind. I call him me.

But at all other times I can feel the mask of the emperor eroding my features: the same mask which set the face of Diocletian at last in that mould of stoney sadness. We are caught in a trap. The emperor is divine. Divinity is beyond feelings and mistakes. We play at gods (I wear a gold-embossed cuirass under my purple cloak) and our subjects play at worshippers. Thus we create each other's dishonesty. I can share a certitude with everyone, because the Augustus is always certain. But my doubts must stay in darkness, and so my own reality becomes elusive to me.

This morning, as I studied the enemy's southern walls, the prefects of the legions posted opposite shuffled about me like slaves. Yes, these men, some of the best and fiercest fighters in the world, had momentarily become slaves. After a while I grew irritated. I decided to test them. I selected the strongest part of the defences: that corner where the amphitheatre looms like a self-contained fort above a whole network of Punic ditches which turn the approach to a foot-soldier's grave.

"We'll attack there," I said.

"Yes, Eternity," replied the prefect of the Primigenia. Only a knotting between the eyes, the slightest squint, betrayed that the man thought I'd gone mad. The other faces were blank.

"That's the easiest salient to attack?" I continued.

"Yes, Augustus."

"Then prepare the men."

But the farce was ended by Gallus Verinus, prefect of the Minervia. That boyish face, aflame with amazement, showed up like a burst of fire in a black wood. Old comrade Verinus, I thank my God for you. He clapped his hand on my shoulder – the sacred shoulder! – and blurted at me: "You'd be mad to try it, Constantine. We'd be cut in pieces!"

The other prefects watched us aghast, as if I'd call down a thunderbolt. But I was starting to enjoy myself. "Prepare your men, Prefect Verinus," I said. "The First Legion Minervia will lead the assault at noon."

It is on such men as Verinus that the Empire was built. He is absolutely fearless. But now, his face crimson with frustration, he dashed his helmet on the ground and bellowed: "I will not lead my men or my Emperor on such a lunacy! Execute me!" Never before had an officer spoken to me like that. I embraced him warmly, to his astonishment. If there is any man I love, it is him.

I first met Verinus when we were boys. His father was an official in the palace at Sirmium and mine was the district governor. I don't recall much about Sirmium, except for huge corridors which shone with torches, miles of them, even by day. I was glad of these. I had a fear of the dark which has never left me.

My mother must have been the first to tell me about the Sun. I recall her holding up a leaf to the light (although I can't remember where or when). "Look at that, Gaius. Look how its veins run! That's the Sun's blood. That's life." Since then I must have sacrificed a thousand times to this Sun Invincible. But to me the great temples seem much like one another, and it's my parents' sacrifices in Illyria that I remember. They worshipped many gods. My father, indeed, was drawn to Syrian and Jewish sects, like the Christians. But only this temple to the Sun-Apollo is sharp in my memory. I think it was in the Dardanian hills, and it was very small, almost rustic. I always felt very proud when we went there. The priests were nervous of my father, who was already prefect of a district. A faint, sweet smell of incense pervaded the place, and because the shrine was in a valley the altar smoke lifted unblown in an immense spiral of blue. But what I remember best is the Sun Himself, shining through the smoke. He hung there rayless like a molten coin, suspended and watching us without benevolence or anger, simply gazing, a god without properties, a god for all time.

That remoteness awed me. I affected to despise my mother's minor deities, because she chattered to them like friends. Their images, with fat bellies and spikey breasts, cluttered the porch of the villa where I was born.

Yet now, confession: I should like to feel the God's hand firm on me. I should like to close my eyes, as my mother did, and sense the closeness of divinity, and my power at one with it. Sometimes in the day this is so. But even then, not always. And at night, never.

Two years ago Apollo granted me a vision in Gaul. I was marching through the country of the Leuci, where his great temple stands. I had just suppressed the rebellion of my own father-in-law, but his blood was not on my hands. He had hanged himself in his own chamber, his face turned black with its tongue sticking out: a bad omen. This temple of Apollo was very grand, as I remember it. The day was hot and the Sun blazed on its walls. I entered the inner court alone. It was built of new stone and dazzled the eyes. Everything quivered and moved. My feet made a strange echo on the pavements. And as I looked up at the face of the god, my stomach emptied. I saw myself looking back at me. His features were my own. He was riding a horse and holding out a laurel. My own divinity was offering a laurel to me. He seemed to smile.

But all my life has been governed by terrible impulses and passions, and when I look back my reason mocks them. So I am unsure now of the man who stood in Apollo's sanctuary then. Did the god really smile?

The trumpets have just sounded the second watch.

Philosophers tell us that we live in a fading cycle and that the virtue is going out of men and of the earth. Others declare that the gods are abandoning us. Perhaps that is why I sometimes feel a gulf open at my feet. I look up at the sky and see the order and invincibility of the Sun. The Sun is pure, absolute. I too, I say, want to be pure: my life, my love, my death. But suddenly, for no reason that I can apprehend, I feel that He is indifferent to me. Not that He has forgotten, but that He never knew. I look around me and all at once I do not see where God is. Then I have a terror that the divine has slipped away and that I am alone. I am His regent, but my mission goes unseen by Him. I fight for unity and order – for what was once 'the immense majesty of the Roman peace' – but the God does not support me.

I begin to be afraid of what I write.

If all this should be for nothing, this march, these deaths . . . ? Today I ordered the execution of two decurions for cowardice. They had followed me through three campaigns on the Rhine. One of them lost his left ear fighting the Bructeri. I saw their expressions as I condemned them.

And here at night, when the skies are empty and the God is sleeping, there is nothing between a man and the cold silence of Infinity. Then I ask myself: does this darkness extend for ever? Will it in the end outlast the Sun? And I find myself trembling. My old tutor used to say that Divinity was light. But one day I found an essay he was reading: the work of some Neoplatonist who wrote that the whole world, and all men, were a dream being dreamt by God. *No*, my tutor had written beneath it. *God is the dream of man.*

I am told the magicians of Maxentius have consecrated me to darkness.

Where is the Sun now? Where is He now?

This is childish, terrible.

V

*The Empress Fausta at Milan, to her cousin
Marina at Nice.*

Yo u cannot imagine, dearest Marina, how tiresome it is to be
the wife of an emperor and yet to have no uses at all. All day
the notables of Milan come to me with petitions, fawning as if we
were long acquaintances. Some of us are. One person wishes to
hear if he will keep his office, another to know if he will receive
it. The latest arrival was a man wanting a monopoly for selling
pigs to the army. I ask you: *Pigs.* These people do not hesitate to
remind me of occasions when my father was alive and we lived in
the imperial palace here. It is astonishing suddenly to hear what a
dear little girl I was. I listen with as much patience as I have (not
much, as you know) then I politely have to remind them that my
husband is busy, a little as if he was an overworked banker. They
depart with ingratitude.

I suppose I should feel relief to be settled again and living in
one place for longer than a day. Our journey over the Alps was
quick and very beautiful, but the road was so bad I felt sick much
of the time and my companion Prisca caught fever. All through
western Cisalpina the wreck of the armies defeated by my
husband went trudging past our carriage: a most pitiful sight.

But here at Milan everything is orderly. The court camp has
just pushed on and joined Gaius at Verona. You've never known
such *bores.* Most of the praetorian tribunes and notaries are
ingratiating and silly, and the camp commandant turned out to
be a Vandal who barely spoke Latin. In fact the only conversation
to be had was that of my husband's Secretary. This is an elderly
Greek called Synesius, who wears his beard long in the old-
fashioned way. The whole camp laughs when they see him walk,
because he's stiff as a log after twelve hours' mule-riding a day;
but there's more brain in that bald head than in a legion of
tribunes. No wonder he is rather paternal, as if he thought the
rest of us children.

And oh, I nearly forgot Hosius. This is a toad dressed up as a
bishop. From Spain, I think. He is all unction and benediction,
and his mule is bent under him like a cradle, poor brute, because

it carries the only fat man in the army. I believe he has attached himself to Gaius as ambassador for the Christians of the northern Empire.

After all this, Mari, you will be surprised to hear that I'd rather be with these people at Verona than sitting in Milan. For one thing I am in a strange position here. Nobody is sure if I support my husband or my brother Maxentius. I can read that question on all their faces. For another thing I hate being absent from the point where issues are decided. You will understand this, you who have known me since we were children. I'm not in the least afraid that Gaius will be killed. Isn't that strange? The death of some people is unimaginable, and my husband is one.

Oh Mari, I do want to be *there*. Did you ever dream, when we played 'mouse' by Lake Verbanus all those years ago, that you were hiding from the future empress of the world? I'm convinced that we receive from childhood the most distorted images. I remember Verbanus always in sunlight. I remember leaves falling like great brown birds from the maple trees. How can I? We were only there in spring.

But one thing I remember true, and so will you. The boy playing with us. The stocky, sneering one you used to call the Dog. My brother Maxentius. Nobody was quite like Maxi even then. How I loathed and adored him!

Childhood is a wretched time.

As people in Gaul first heard what he was doing in Rome – the numbers of men killed and women raped – they were all incredulous. All, that is, except me. I knew that it was true. When I was seven I had a kitten and it disappeared. I've never told anybody this. I searched everywhere for it. At last I went to the back of the palace baths, and there I found it, nailed to the ground through its eyes. Around it ten or fifteen other small animals lay strangled or impaled. That was Maxi's garden.

I think my values cruelly unpredictable. Since then, in Rome, my brother has murdered three of my friends. Each crime has outraged me, then I have forgotten it. *But the kitten's murder went unforgiven for ever.*

Dear Marina, I have only you left in whom to confide. I do this freely because I am sure of your trust, but please destroy this letter after reading it, as you have destroyed the others. Anyway, reading old letters is a melancholy pastime. All the way over the

Alps in my closed carriage to Turin I had for companion only sick Prisca and a casket of old papers from which I dare not be parted. So I dosed Prisca and read the papers.

What should I find but the bundle of letters written me by Gaius when he was away on campaign! Did I ever tell you that he fell in love with me in the second year of our marriage? I unrolled them and started to read. I felt my throat turning dry, and I blushed redder than Prisca for all her fever. Listen: '*Secret of my life, little dove, great miracle — how I long for you! My impatience to return is driving a whole army like a flail. Yes, it's a terrible weapon, this army driven by you! Oh Fausta beloved, how I ache to take that radiant face to my lips! Can I kiss you through a letter? I kiss you, I kiss you. Open those dark eyes. I kiss them too. Yes, sitting in this empty tent I touch you. I run my fingers over your shoulders, the little blue veins of them. . . . (Don't mock me.) And don't forget, Faustina, that beauty in this world is the shadow of an upper glory, that when we gaze on one another we gaze through each to heaven, that when I kiss your lips (sweet lips!) I am kissing the Eternal. For "the Eternal and the Beautiful are One"* [he quotes Plotinus]. *Through Eros we are one, my dove, my beautiful. Perfect, Always, One.*'

How insane it is! (I *order* you to burn this letter.) I remember him returning too, looking as he does now: very tall and — yes — handsome, with that intense face of powerful bones. If there was such a thing as a golden time, I suppose that year was ours. I almost persuaded myself that I was capable of love. (You long ago guessed that his passion made me afraid.) But in our lighter times of laughter, of teasing, I could think: I love him, this is love. That was the year of those receptions in the palace at Treves, when you and Lucullus came. I make no secret to you (you know it anyway): I am terribly vain. Sitting beside him in that gold-embroidered dress you so much envied, I felt myself on Olympus. Of course you thought me conceited. So I was. So I am. I'm married to the Sun.

But I was always terrified of burning.

Isn't it ridiculous, then, that these letters now sear my heart?

Enough. I'm growing maudlin, and must end. By the way, a past friend sends you her respects; she's my new companion, the Lady Politta. You knew her as Livilla Anulina. She's as plump as a partridge now, and going on forty.

My regards to your Lucullus, and my love to you.

VI

Journal-Memoir of Constantine.

26 August

[*In the hand of Synesius.*]

MORNING: the last earthworks are dug. We hold Verona in a ring of steel and will in time suffocate her. The catapults have opened up all along our lines. So far the walls blister but do not crack. It seems they were built in eight months by the Emperor Gallienus. They are therefore quite modern, and are exceedingly strong.

Towards ten o'clock one of the southern gates showed unexpected signs of weakness, but it is defended by a deep ditch; this forces an oblique approach which exposes to the ramparts the men's sword-arms instead of their shields. An ancient trick. Where is a left-handed legion?

Sapping continues against the northern walls. Mobile towers near completion. At eleven o'clock the Ulpia Victrix sent in battering-rams at two points by the river, hoping to breach the outworks. But the God judged otherwise. Our iron-plated screens failed us. A few casualties.

At noon I attended sacrifice to the Sun Invincible. Something tight and cold inside my chest all the time. The augurs reported that the heifer's liver was half eaten away. They gave contradictory readings on this, none of them favourable. The practices of Maxentius never leave my mind. They say that all his life he has destroyed his rivals by consecrating them to the gods of the underworld.

Last night I had a vivid dream. A woman came and stood beside my bed – a middle-aged woman weeping and protesting. This provoked a furious anger in me. I said: 'It's no time for tears' and struck her. She immediately vanished.

I submitted this dream to the *haruspices*. Their interpretation was this: the woman is Rome, sad for the afflictions of the tyrant; I struck away her sorrow.

Afternoon: completed pontoon bridge at the ford; consulted maps with the praetorian prefect and staff. Plans for marching on Aquileia, on Modena. Verinus tells me a strange story. As an officer in Syria he was detailed to recover treasure pilfered from the temple of the Sun-Jupiter in Damascus. He found the robbers wandering in the desert, driven mad by sunstroke, their faces swollen like flowers. With such a guardian, how can we fail? It is insane to think that there is anything more potent than the symbol which the God has so manifestly set before us in the skies.

Now that Verona is encircled I have written to the Empress, who has left Turin against my orders, either to return there or to join us here at once. I believe it is safer here than in Milan.

[*Constantine continues in his own hand.*]

There is selfishness in this, I know. I want her by me. Perhaps I've come to rely too much on her. Or perhaps it is simply that I can be myself with her. No play-acting, no infallible Augustus there! I lay at her feet too long to pretend to be more than a man.

But sometimes the remembered sweetness of her puts me in a rage and I don't understand what has happened to us. Just as in the first year of our marriage I saw a girl – a haughty, abstracted girl – so now, on the farther side of love, I see a woman, a totally self-sufficient woman.

But in between – did I dream it?

I recall the day, even the hour, when my eyes were opened – or closed. It was at a banquet in Treves. A very ordinary banquet. Fausta does not even remember it, except for the end. I must have held it as a celebration, because I had returned that same afternoon from a four-month tour of Upper Germany. The Empress, I heard, had been ill; but she would attend that evening. It was early winter. We'd had heating installed under the porphyry floors of the antiquated palace, and the dining-hall was suffocating, filled with smoke and the smell of saffron. I quite forget who else was present. Fausta reclined next to me in a dark dress. We'd seen little of each other since that political convenience which was our marriage. She had shared my bed perhaps a dozen times, and suffered a miscarriage. It seems inexplicable to me now that I could have been so indifferent and so incurious of her. While some palace orator read a eulogy, I remember closing my eyes (this is interpreted as ecstasy) and wondering how my men were faring on the Rhine – it had been snowing heavily for days.

The banquet dragged. Used for four months to the plain fare of

19

military stations, the food disgusted me. A wild boar stuffed with roast dormice is vivid in my mind. And marinated song-birds sent from Cyprus. After a while I became aware of a faint, elusive scent. She told me later that it was sweet calamus, and I've never smelt it since without a pang. I opened my eyes and saw that she had leant closer to me. The orator had finished. She said: "You're tired."

For the first time since my return, I noticed her. She looked maturer than I remembered. I thought: she's been sick. But her talk was animated and even seemed tender. She asked me how cold our march had been, how far a cohort could travel in deep snow. And was it true that one year the cavalry of the Bructeri had crossed the Rhine on solid ice with their heavy wagons, cattle and families all together?

As she questioned me, I realised that I did not know her at all, that I had never known her. I was reclining beside a stranger: a woman of twenty-one in whose pale face the bones were delicate and fine. The dark silk dress showed off arms and shoulders of almost translucent whiteness. Silvery nails completed the slenderness of her hands, and her forearms were clouded by a faint softness of hair, like the fur of an animal. Her body looked lithe, finely-strung: what the Persians call a watchful body. She had (and still has) the small, even teeth which so many of our Roman women lack. Why, I wondered, had I not admired her before? But even her hair looked different. It fell down in ringlets in the old Flavian way – a rich, brown, barbarian head of hair for which the women of Italy would have given their eyes. And once, when she leant forward, the neck of her dress hung fractionally loose and I glimpsed, with all the guilt of an adulterer, the gentle swell of breasts above her corslet.

As she talked I became aware of a strange lightness stirring under my ribs. She touched the new scar on my neck – she'd noticed it immediately – and inquired about an old one in my thigh. I thought: I only mentioned that old wound to her once, but she's remembered.

Yes, it seems odd to me now, but I thought of her as tender. I noticed the way her lips tilted up at the corners; and above all her eyes, dark and arresting, wide-spaced. Her whole face was filled with animation, at once radiant, intense and slightly solemn. Looking back I can see that she was perfectly controlled whereas I, who had commanded armies, suddenly could not command my tongue or even the trembling of my hands.

Many courses of food came and went. I barely touched them. The wine I did not touch at all. Fausta ate artichoke-hearts with cat-like motions of her head. A lyre-player sang; I never heard him. An official toasted the Emperor and the army. I barely raised my eyes from my wife – I think I had forgotten who the Emperor was.

An hour later several of my generals were badly drunk. This is something I have always frowned upon at official banquets. I am considered puritan, I know, but the sight of middle-aged men, schooled in a hard discipline, vomiting and roaring and pawing their women is something I regret. This time, for a while, I ignored it. We were all recovering from a long starvation: from woman-hunger in particular. But the dry, salt desserts had done their worst, and the men began drinking to get drunk. Several were already snoring where they lay, the garlands askew across their throats. The air stifled. I remember how unreal the other women appeared to me that night with their high, tinkling laughs and the little taught gestures of their fingers. More like collections of jewellery they seemed, with faces gone dim between the embroidered necks of their dalmatics and the gold bands in their hair. The only living thing in the whole room was the vivid, serious face of the woman by my side.

After a display of clowning by a troupe of Spanish acrobats I stood up and very abruptly (it was later intimated) dismissed the company. It used to be unheard-of for anybody to depart before the Emperor and Empress, but since I remained engrossed in talk with Fausta the palace slaves were eventually left with the strange sight of the rulers of northern Europe reclining alone amongst a litter of spittle and bones. Soon the slaves themselves retired confused, whispering. Our voices broke on silence. Fausta kept shifting her feline body on the couch and looking at me questioningly.

I forget with what stumbling words I told her I loved her. My own wife! But I remember the alarmed whisper with which she answered "Love?" Then she touched her hand against her forehead, peering at me from beneath it as if the angle of her arm were a shield. She was frightened and astonishingly beautiful. Her eyes had turned moist, so that I thought she was going to cry.

They shone strangely. And a blush was moving along her cheek-bones, high up in the pallor of the skin. She was like a newly-discovered land, virgin, startled.

I ask myself now: why do I write this down? Perhaps the answer is this: words continue to contain what we have lost. I embalm her, like an Egyptian queen, thus.

[*From the Commonplace Book of Synesius.* . . . I sometimes feel the Augustus wants to possess for ever those times when (he believes) he touches on the divine — in achievement, in love, in experience of every kind. This stems, I think, from a deep void in him.

I find that I can admire and dislike a quality at the same time. Especially in Fausta. That aloofness, that self-containment. Compared to those fortifications the walls of Verona are toys! How I loved them, hate them.

Fausta.

Some madness lingers. I don't see vices in you, but absences.

Last winter, while we walked in the palace peristyle, I took a handful of snow and pressed it against her cheek. I said: "That's your love." Cold. And she smiled (she actually *smiled*!) and said "Yes."

VII

Hosius, Bishop of Cordoba, to Victor of Ulia,
Priest.

Verona, 27 August

GREETINGS, my dearest Victor, and to our brothers in Christ, my blessing.

You cannot imagine what a country God has created here. Never has a quartermaster had so easy a task feeding an army! The harvest is in. Every kind of cereal and vegetable is stored in the barns, and many fruits.

As to Verona, it is built half of pink marble, and sits in the elbow of a fine river. All around it our siege-works are truly terrifying. The men of this army are the tallest I have ever seen, and savage. I can barely understand what many of them say, for

22

they are mostly Gauls, Germans and Britons. Their dialect sounds like stones grating together. The German auxiliaries have kept their own uniforms and standards. The Gepidae even wear trousers and ride their horses clutching little shields painted with barbaric devices. But I suppose these tribes to be safe recruits for our armies, since they hate each other more than they hate us.

It will not surprise you that Christians are few among such men. Their deities mean little more to them than charms. Of humility or penitence they understand nothing at all. I spent this morning at the bedside of a Gaulish centurion dying of an arrow wound. I spoke to him for a long time of the Holy Mysteries and he agreed at last to be baptised. Then he died, calling on Epona the horse-goddess. That is the kind of people these are.

But they have one object of veneration at least more worthy than demons – the noble Augustus. In the army the cult of emperor-worship, godless though it may be, is less stifling than in our native Spain. For here the object of their prayers is amongst them, and is a magnificent-looking man. Powerfully built he is, with a close-cropped auburn beard. Now thirty-two (an age when most men's features begin to fill) he shows a strong-boned and intemperate face. When I talk to him I watch both his eyes and his hands. The first are grey and searching; they are not happy. The second start twisting together the moment he's impatient.

Among the soldiers countless stories are told about him. They say he's able to be in many places at once, and that he never sleeps – or rather that he sleeps on his feet, like a horse. The truth is that he's a masterly organiser. He applies his mind fiercely to a problem until he has worried an answer out of it. Then he executes his will with astonishing vigour and speed.

Many people are frightened of him. They say he's austere and ruthless. And certainly it is important to approach him with great diplomacy. He can be most tempestuous. But I myself have been treated kindly by him ever since I joined the court this spring. I spoke to him then of Constantius his father, whose goodwill to the Christians was alone unblemished among all the Caesars of his time. And as you can imagine, dear brother in Christ, I almost wept when I told him what I'd suffered in the great persecution, and how his father's clemency alone ordered my release.

23

The Augustus is easily angered but quickly kind. He noticed my emotion and gave me a most gentle audience. During the persecution in the East I'd often praised the way he continued his father's tolerance towards us, and now I boldly added that the Church had emerged innocent and victorious from its travails. His expression held no threat.

Several times since then we've spoken together, and I feel I am secured in his trust. By the grace of God those around him do not seem prejudiced against us, although even to this there is one perhaps comical exception – his personal servant Cecrops. This is an Illyrian veteran who has known the Augustus from childhood. He's very old now, but still strong. His whole head is a cloud of white hair, and he curses even prefects and tribunes who visit the Augustus at inconvenient times. Yesterday he said to me (fingering my robes): "You bishops, you live off your flock like other shepherds. But what wolves do you scare?"

I imagine the Augustus is almost equally ignorant of our habits and doctrine. I have no way of telling. One may not approach him on such a subject. But he is, beneath his majesty, a rather uneducated man. Certainly he has no conception that the path to God is through humility.

This letter goes by my slave Dion, one of the faithful. May God preserve you, beloved brother.

VIII

The Empress Fausta to Constantine Augustus at Verona.

Milan, 28 August

MOST Noble Husband,
You say that I am indispensable to you. How have I so reduced you? Besides, self-deceiving Gaius, reflect that you have dispensed with me for eight weeks and have since subdued half Cisalpine Gaul. I, meanwhile, have received the Spanish embassies and reorganised the palace at Arles. Separated, we achieve.

You ask that either I join you at Verona or return to the safety of Turin. I cannot be both wolf and chicken, you say. But you know well enough that I am wolf. Perhaps you're right that Milan may not always be safe for me. And I shouldn't care to fall into the hands of my brother. I might even be forced to say things. Maxi was always very good at getting people to say things. Even as a boy – and boys are all detestable – he was a remarkable torturer.

So I will leave for Verona in the morning. I will limit my household to the numbers you ask. Yes, I will be good. My retinue, in façt, is already much reduced. I have been dropping servants – ill or dead – all the way from Arles to here, and apart from my companion I have no more than a handful of slaves and eunuchs, with a single seamstress and hairdresser. My new companion, Livilla Politta, is unremarkable, except for silliness. I hope the tribunes of the court camp will not find her attractive. Her looks, I suspect, conform to military taste. But I must have her with me. I am not going to be the only woman (except for prostitutes) in the army of the Augustus.

Don't fret about my journey. (Your letter sounded agitated.) Of course my guard will accompany me, although my protection has always been the terror of your name.

I am bringing you a present: boots of Ligurian leather, beautifully made.

IX

Journal-Memoir of Constantine.

30 August

I BEGAN today full of hope. The enemy sallied out in an effort to destroy the catapults of the Primigenia – a sign of anxiety. They became entangled in their own ditches then retreated before reaching our breastworks, leaving their dead. An hour later a letter arrived by imperial courier from Milan to say that the Empress is coming.

That is the end of the day's good fortune. A series of messages has reached me from the Master of the Offices. It is now certain that the enemy general Pompeianus slipped out of the city before our encirclement was complete, and is gathering forces around Aquileia. And the news from Rome horrifies. The tyrant's practices shake the skies. He has ripped open pregnant women and offered up their unborn infants, inspecting the entrails for an augury. In one the intestines were found to be black or monstrously distended (the reports varied). This child's body was marked with my name and that of Fausta, and was sewn back into the womb. That night it was buried under the Capitoline Hill, and so we were dedicated to the gods of the nether world.

These horrors threw me into the blackest state. The morning, I know, was bright and sunlit, yet it seemed as if a glaze had settled over the whole land. Was there something wrong with my eyes? The movements of men and horses looked senseless, like those of mice in cages. Shadows were more real than the objects which threw them. The very air threatened. I went to my rooms and had my face bathed and anointed. My head was throbbing. When I emerged again nothing had changed. The light fell full overhead, but the earth lay opaque. I must have groaned out loud because one of my staff tribunes asked: "Is my lord well?"

I said: "Who is unwell?" I summoned the prefects of the legions. My head cleared but my mind remained heavy. We prepared against the reinforcements of Pompeianus: plans for new earthworks facing outward. The labour and tedium of these precautions showed on every face. As for digging, the ground is still hard after the hot summer. It was then that the fate of the Emperor Probus flickered into my mind: murdered by his men after overworking them. I could not banish this abstruse thought. When I rode along the lines of the Minervia and the legionaries clambered onto the breastworks to cheer me, I felt a profound relief. This shows how overwrought I was. It must never happen again.

It was now almost noon. The Sun had hazed. I found myself watching the sky. My gloom had given way to nervousness. I know this mood. I have felt it on the evening before battles. It gives a feeling of physical frailty. At such times omens multiply: unforeseen noises, the trajectory of a bird. The God is holding His breath, or so it seems, and my senses are sharpened to receive it. I have learnt that this is not a mood easily shared, and I have never issued commands at such times. Everything is too uncertain. One must simply wait, and listen.

But today, because I was depressed, I summoned Gallus Verinus to me. He was covered in dust by the men's digging. We rode a short way beyond camp, followed by the standard of his legion and by some twenty of my staff. I said suddenly: "We'll go and sacrifice at the Altar of the Sun in Segnus." He looked at me nonplussed. Segnus was a shrine-village two miles to the west. I had never been there myself. It was just a name.

Verinus said in his direct way: "Why there?" I had never before left the army for such a reason. "What's wrong with the priests of the sacred retinue?" he went on. "Give them something to do. They're idle as tortoises." I didn't answer. I didn't know what was wrong with them. But Verinus was undeterred by my grimness. He kept slapping his hip in boyish high spirits. "Don't worry. Whatever it is, it'll be all right. Let things take their course. Don't force them. The gods are good." He chattered on. "I tell you, there's no soldier in the army, not one, who doesn't expect to be in Rome by winter, warming his body on the ladies of the Subura." All the pleasure of the God was shining in this man. I kept him close to me, boot to boot, as if I might catch the rays of his delight like a fever. For the past weeks I've known that vigour and radiance in my own body. Why has it gone now?

He hadn't been to Rome since childhood, Verinus said, but he'd heard that the women of the Viminal and Aventine were beautiful. I said I'd heard the Aventine was a slum.

"Oh no, Augustus," he answers, "I have the address of a perfect woman there, a patrician, given me by Sacrovir. He says she's not yet married, and that her breasts hang quite perfect, like pomegranates."

I asked: "How does Sacrovir know about her breasts?"

Verinus looked puzzled, then laughed. "You're right. I think the Aventine is a slum. But the women of the Viminal. . . ."

And so he talked light-heartedly, while I sometimes listened, until Segnus came in sight. The idea of sacrificing here had struck me with such force and suddenness that I felt sure it was the prompting of the God. I was filled with expectancy. A messenger had preceded us, and the few villagers were clustered at the temple's entrance. As soon as they saw me they fell on their stomachs.

The shrine turned out to be small and derelict. Two elderly

priests awaited us. They kept wringing their hands and glancing at one another. The senior tried to greet me, but stammered uncontrollably and kissed my hand. They had had no time even to garland the altar.

But we stood before it solemnly. I asked for the mantle. The older priest's face went ashen with apology as he handed it to me – stained and crumpled – but it would have been worse for anyone to have mentioned it. My retinue averted their eyes as I put it on. The other priest led forward the sheep to be slaughtered. It was a sad-looking creature. We watched it for any ominous movement, but it came docilely. So inured were the priests to the meaning of their incantations that even now they chanted them like Nubian spells. Their two quavering voices interwove with an unbearable melancholy. I took the knife. The sheep died without sound and left a colourless trickle of blood which barely stained my hands. As an augury, it meant nothing. I offered this poor sacrifice to the God and waited for a sign. There was silence. The wind had fallen. The sky spread above us in a passive roof of blue. Although the dedicatory prayer had long ago left my lips, I continued to gaze at the Sun.

It is only this evening, sitting in quiet, that I recognise a strangeness in my own desire. It is this: I have lost my fear of evil omens. At that moment, instead, I was like a neglected child who prefers harshness to indifference. *I simply wanted any sign at all*.

But the God sent none. Verinus told me afterwards that I was glowering with anger and frustration all the time, so I suppose this must be true. But my inmost feeling was loneliness. Afterwards I went into the sanctuary. The cult at this temple must be almost dead, because my feet left their prints in thick dust and there was a smell of bats' urine. I was quite alone. I advanced to the statue of Apollo. Its paint was flaking and the obsidian of one eye had fallen or been plucked out. The other eye glared at me. I thought with shame: the gods repay our neglect in kind. But I was loath to go. I thought of my army and of our uncertain future. And I think of it now. I remembered too the dream of Aurelian and the pious men of my Illyrian homeland – a single God in heaven, whose regent is a single emperor on earth. Desperation urged me to speak. I steeled myself.

"Mighty and invincible Sun!" My voice sounded huge. "Dispel the darkness!"

Almost at once, and before the boom of my voice had faded, I became aware of movement in the sanctuary. I looked up. The whole ceiling was stirring and shifting. I stared in astonishment as it began to flake away in black gusts. Next moment the tiny faces of sick monkeys were fanning round my head on jagged wings, and the air sang with an unearthly, echoless screaming.

I've seen men die in every agony, I've held snakes in my hands and eaten scorpions in the desert, and none of this has touched me. But I'm horrified by bats.

We rode back in silence. I felt utter emptiness. Only once Verinus patted my horse's mane as if he was comforting me, and said: "I told those priests to clean their temple."

As we neared Verona it became clear that the news of enemy reinforcements mustering in the east had spread. The whole of the court camp was moving inside the earthworks. I looked for our priests or for any voice dressed as authority. I am ashamed that I needed such comfort. But huge dust clouds obliterated anything not close at hand, and the efforts of orderlies and slaves to clear a path for us increased the confusion. Verinus pointed out the Bishop of Cordoba, who was ordering his servants off the road ahead. Among his own people, I noticed, the prelate looked ebullient and self-confident, whereas to me he shows a more ingratiating face. But the plump good-nature of this person attracted me today. I motioned him to ride beside me, which he did most uncomfortably on a white mule. I told him where I had been, and added belligerently: "God infuses the Sun. It's the living symbol of the power of Him."

Hosius bowed his head, which for some reason irritated me. He is balding. I insisted on a reply, and was astonished when he licked his lips, clearly afraid of what he was about to say. The courage of a timid man is always moving. One doesn't find much of that kind in the army. "Forgive me, Augustus," he answered, "but your Sun is silent. He does not speak."

I heard Verinus' harness clinking uneasily behind me. I demanded: "You people deny the Sun?"

The bishop was not discouraged. The angry pressure which I felt around my throat and jaw was evidently invisible. "No, Eternity. Our own Christ is called the Sun of Righteousness – but he speaks."

I demanded: "How?"

But then the bishop started to interpret his books. Why do priests always talk in riddles and mysteries? I lack patience for these sophisms. I only know what is in me, and what I am. I sent him away.

This evening I questioned the Sacred Consistory about the religious practices of our army in the field. Is there anything we are omitting? Are the offerings as plentiful as is customary? Is their quality similar? But it appears that all these things are precisely the same as before. Nothing has changed since the days of our German victories, and the High Priest seemed offended by my questions. "The God attends my Lord," he said, as if the God was obliged to do so.

Tonight, for more than an hour, I've sat in silence. I've emptied my mind, even of anguish. I've waited to know what to do.

What has fallen between myself and Him? Why am I abandoned at the crux? Why? It is hard to write my fear. To write it makes it real.

But write it.

Perhaps divinity is *somewhere else*. Perhaps *I am alone*. Yet even as I think this something in me says No! No! It's impossible that . . . [there follows a passage which is erased] . . . lie that 'the Sun doesn't speak.' He must be either angry or He is waiting. Is the God angry? He must be angry. I pray He is angry.

Resolution: I will endure this as long as it lasts. I will act as I have always done, out of experience and my mind's clarity.

So this polluted day ends.

X

The Lady Livilla Politta to the
Lady Lucia Balba at Turin.

25th Milepost west of Verona, 2 September

DEAREST Biji, the most appalling thing has happened. We are going to join the *army*. It is most unexpected and absolutely *terrifying*. As you can imagine I don't know anything about the army or what it does. I promised the Empress that I'd be her companion until *death*. But I thought we were staying in Milan.

As it is we are already almost at Verona and keep passing the most dreadful sights along the way. We travel in a huge *carruca* with little talc windows so that nobody can see in. And I can't tell you how many slaves are with us, *hundreds* I should think, with our wardrobes following behind somewhere. And as if this were not enough we have sixty bodyguards. Their commander rides near our carriage and reminds me of my poor, dear Cornelius to look at. I nearly cried. But his soldiers are all giants of men, *horribly* handsome.

As to the Empress, I confess I absolutely *adore* her. I can't remember anybody who struck me so forcibly. She has the most beautiful dark eyes. Her face is too thin, I think, but she must be very tired, poor dear. And of course she is not at all patrician. She can only speak a very broken Greek and her manners are much too self-conscious to be good. Do you know the family? Illyrian, naturally, and I believe absolutely *nobody* a generation ago. (I expect you realise she was only the granddaughter of Diocletian by adoption?) Actually she has such beautiful skin you'd think her Macedonian, and I even mentioned this to her. My dear, a terrible blunder. Apparently the Illyrians and Macedonians hate one another. I didn't know.

I *do* like her but I don't feel I *know* her. She's so vivid and intelligent, yet somehow *cool*. Very much the empress. And she takes it quite for granted that we should be going to the siege of Verona, just as if it was Baiae. I can't understand it. She doesn't seem to consider that we might both be killed. And when you think that I received the prefect of Verona at my house only last month! A charming old man, who knew about wines. Oh how *grotesque* it all is, don't you think?

Above all, what do you imagine it must be like to be *her*? Her husband and brother fighting one another! What would *you* do? I haven't dared even speak of it to her. She's only mentioned Maxentius once and that was with revulsion. But it was unnerving to hear her sound so *familiar* about him. She calls him Maxi. It sent shivers all through me. She spoke of him as 'that little pig', which I thought rather an understatement.

This evening we've been deciding what clothes we shall wear for our arrival in Verona tomorrow. I've never *seen* such a wardrobe as hers. You'd give your fingers for it. She became quite girlish and excited. But I find her attitudes to dress curious. It's as if she wishes to be beautiful, but not to *attract*. She makes her face up that way too, without emphasising her lips, and she heightens its pallor with cumin. Rather austere for so young a woman.

I must stop now, my dear, because I want to send this to you by *imperial courier*. You'll be the most wanted woman in Turin!

XI

Journal-Memoir of Constantine.

3 September

I'VE written orders twice that the Empress return to Turin, but have sent neither. And now she is here. In mid-afternoon the fanfare greeting her arrival could be heard along all our southern entrenchments, and the men cheered, because they love audacity. I did not go to her at once, but waited for her household to settle, and rode over in the early evening with a small retinue. There followed one of those ceremonies which I so detest. Her bodyguard, the Sacred Consistory and the whole travelling court were there to witness our reunion. Such a clashing of javelins, grovelling of eunuchs and braying of mules that neither of us heard anything the other said. But our every blink was recorded.

It was eight weeks since I'd seen her. She appeared to stand a little isolated in her retinue, and despite her slenderness she seemed to dominate it. We greeted each other formally. I always watch the first smile; it is often the only honest one. Fausta's showed pleasure but a certain uneasy reserve. She looked pale with travel. In fact this watching for the smile is unnecessary with her. She will be cruel rather than lie. I gave her my arm and led her into the only built accommodation in the camp: a dowdy villa vacated by the praetorian prefect. I remember, for some reason, the way her hand rested on mine as we walked: the long, regal delicacy of it, touching but not holding. We didn't look at one another.

Her servants had already feminised the villa. Silks and cushions were piled about its couches and the rooms were filled with the odour of musk. Nothing could have less resembled our dark, grandiose reception rooms at Treves, yet I felt just as if I had returned to her from campaign, instead of she to me. Her slave-women were demure and excited. The atmosphere was all of gentleness and sanity. Fausta had brought me many little gifts. I sat in a high-backed chair and received them. This has become a ritual on my homecomings. She gave these presents, as she always does, with an air of disparagement, almost of recoil. But she was pleased by my gratitude. I watched her face: the white lift of cheekbones and the calm lips. Her eyes settled on me very straight, wanting to know what I was thinking, but perhaps not wanting to be left alone with me. It was hard to tell.

A woman lingered after I'd ordered the rest to go. Fausta introduced her as the Lady Politta: a vapid creature with fluffy yellow hair. I remembered her as the subject of a state security report. I told her to leave us.

I think my manner may often be rude, but nobody ever tells me so, except Fausta. "You shouldn't have shouted at her like that." (Did I shout?) "She's nervous. And I've given her a good opinion of you." She was smiling at something. "She lives for us to enter Rome."

"Why is that?" I asked. "Does she hate your brother? Has she suffered in these wars?"

"Oh no. She wants to visit a scent shop by the Temple of Flora."

We burst into laughter. I stood up and clasped Fausta against me, cursing my armour. I could not feel her at all. I was suddenly relieved to have her here. I held her away from me and stared into her face, looking for something I don't know. She stared back in the vivid and direct way which assures me of her integrity. I can look at her and ask anything. The face is not always friendly, but it is never false. If she does not understand, she says she does not understand. She does not say "Of course, Eternity." If she disapproves she says she disapproves. She doesn't say "Naturally, Augustus."

She pushed me away and sat down. "What's wrong with you? Something's wrong. You look starved."

She sounded rather irritated. I went to the wall-mirror behind me, and stared in it. I expected to see one face, but saw another.

33

Yes, its flesh – there is little enough – was dragged down about the mouth and knotted between the eyes. It was hard, grim and pained.

I did not know how to express myself to Fausta. I strode up and down. I did not mention Maxentius. But I admitted to my disappointment at the temple of Segnus. I had expected a sign from the God and he had sent a flock of bats. I grew angry as I talked of it. We were approaching the crisis of the siege and the God had sent bats! Then I started to malign the priests of my retinue. They were inept and ignorant, I said. I did not say what they were ignorant of. I did not know. But I declared that there was nobody but them to consult, because my secretariat could not voice an opinion on a syntax let alone a god, and the Master of the Offices devoted himself to the discovery of bad news. I was surprised at my bitterness and dimly aware of its injustice, which made me angrier still. My civil court officials are scrupulous and hard-working, otherwise they would not still be there. They have not changed. I have not changed.

Fausta held my wrist to stop me striding about. She said: "What about Synesius?"

I said: "Synesius believes in nothing." I thought of him at that moment with hot dislike. As a Master he is invaluable, and his intelligence and learning far surpass mine. I'm prepared to consult him about anything – except what is sacred. On this he is like a dead man. There was once a time when I did ask him, and that parched face and those grey lips gave such answers as I've never forgotten. In the old days there were many like him: Epicureans, Cynics and such. But not any more.

"There's something eerie in Synesius," I said. Sometimes when I'm with him a peculiar image enters my mind: an Egyptian papyrus scroll. Yes, his wisdom comes from another age, whose hieroglyphs are now forgotten. When he dies, there will be no more Synesiuses. But he's a good Secretary.

I could feel Fausta's gaze on me, a little frustrated. She likes to be definite, but did not know what to say. She follows religious custom. Her people worshipped Jupiter and Hercules. I had not meant to talk to her like this. These last days I've had such a feeling of inner frailty, my stomach might be glass. I can't predict myself and must step carefully and not alarm her.

But I realise, stronger now, my need for her. Among the

vapour of all my wary, flattering or frightened subjects, she is solid. I began complaining to her about this, too: the cringing of those around me.

She said: "You create their cringing, Gaius. You're intolerant." She laughed. "Like me."

I said: "When people kneel I trample on them. Is it my fault they kneel?"

She said: "Yes."

I scowled at her but she laughed back at me. It was impossible to be hard with her, since we were discussing my tyranny. I said morosely: "And who suffers more than I do? I need to whet my mind on men, but this way I'm blunted. I don't know myself. You tell me that I shouted at the Lady Politta just now. But I promise you I was *absolutely unaware* of shouting. I probably shout at everybody. All the time. Nobody tells me."

Fausta said suddenly: "You must keep your head, Gaius. You haven't done wrong. That isn't why the God is silent. It's the Fates, that's all. You must wait."

She sat so possessed, so contained. The paradox of us, smothered for a while, reared up and hurt me. I wanted to dissect her, divide her into what was sometimes mine and what was inalienably hers. For the thousandth time she baffled me. Her warmth of mind, her concern for me, shone unmistakably in those intense dark eyes. But something else in her imposed an unchanging distance between us. I even tried, looking at her, to detect where the coldness was lodged. If not in the eyes, then where? It seemed to centre in her high cheek-bones; and in the lips perhaps, too thin. But when I looked again all this had changed, and the warmth and coldness of her were compounded once more into a face of maddening uniqueness – an enigma of which she is quite unaware.

Perhaps it was to hurt her that I started talking about Maxentius. More likely it was to lay my fear at her feet. At first she was composed, but as I went on a stony expression came over her and she pressed her fingertips together in her lap in a way I've come to know. Little by little, although I hadn't meant to, I told her everything. These monsters dropped from my mouth one by one. In the daylight sanity of that room they were, for me, momentarily exorcised. But Fausta's fingers, pressed together, showed pale with tension. When I talked about the newborn infants she dug her hands into her lap to stop them trembling.

I said: "You know him. You think this is true?"

She said: "Yes."

"And the children ripped open?"

"Yes." She clenched her fists and cried suddenly: "Gaius, you don't understand him! He's capable of anything! Don't keep asking me could he do this or that! He's not you. He'd drink from the rivers of Hell." She started up and walked with nervous paces, crossing among the chairs and the couches, back again. "We'll have to endure him."

Her anxiety had turned me calm. I came and stood behind her, and soothed her shoulders in my hands. "Don't tremble." I said to her the words which I should long ago have said to myself. "Nothing's going to touch us. His demons can't save him. I'd wager a Gaulish legionary against a demon!" But my laughter sounded formal. "There's no army your brother can field which mine will not destroy. These men are fit to rout the Great King of Persia. They're hard as iron, and they love me."

Fausta seemed not to have heard. She neither leant against me nor stepped away. She might have forgotten I was there. Her voice was pensive and bitter: "He writes our names in innocent blood. He wants to damn us." I've noticed before, when she talks of Maxentius (which is not often) that she sometimes lapses into children's language. And now she spat: "*The little beast, the traitor*", which sounded ridiculous in her dark, mature voice.

The word traitor struck me. I said: "What did you two do together, when you were children? So different from one another."

"We were not different," she said. "I was his slave, that's all." She glanced at me. "You look surprised that I could be a slave. But I was. I was his rebellious shadow – that's what he called me. Maxi had extraordinary power, as a child. In fact, I never thought of him as a child at all, and he never was. He's never been an adult either. He would laugh at both adults and children. It was as if he came from somewhere else."

"Where else?"

"If you don't understand I can't explain," she said impatiently. "You ask what did we do? We played like other children. But we were not exactly like other children. We seemed to be, but we weren't. We used to hurt and bewilder

36

the others. They were our enemies. I remember. . . . But I don't want to talk about it. It's finished.''

I said: "Tell me.''

"But you can't understand, Gaius.'' Her gaze had shifted from me. She added with an intense, secret remembrance: "We were animals. You never ran wild as we did.''

"You talk as if you loved him.''

She said: "I hate him.''

As I write I think how strange it is that this woman and I, both born of emperors, should have lived such disparate childhoods. When I received her in marriage from that old barbarian of a father, I never guessed what life the defiant-looking girl had lived. As for me, I had hardened out my adolescence in the roving court of Diocletian. Oh the fabled beauties of that court! What rubbish! Fans and fingernails and weak smiles are all my memory, not so much people as ghostly flirtations, whose hair was blonded with *Spuma Batava* and skins reeked of nard. But Fausta cuts to the heart. She's Illyrian, like me. Total, immediate. I suppose we're an exacting people.

I asked her why Maxentius did not march against me himself, why he skulked in Rome neglecting his best general. Was he frightened?

"Frightened?'' She went into a long, soft peal of laughter. "He's just *lazy*.''

It was uncanny how she knew. And I am sure she did. When she spoke about this man she became half strange to me. As I looked at her, a thought distorted my mind. It's been known in our time for relatives or lovers to secure their victims by sorcery. The closer the two have been, the easier it is. But this fantasy vanished with her renewed attentiveness. She asked me a crowd of questions: about Turin and Brescia, about the siege, about the battle beyond the ford. She wanted to know the mood of the army, the names of tribunes killed, details of my health, what and how much we were eating, together with twenty or thirty other matters, and Oh had I noticed, when crossing the Alps, a beautiful wild cyclamen?

She stood up and threw off her travelling cloak. Underneath she wore a green dalmatic, very high at the neck, aggressively chaste. It is astonishing that after five years of marriage my hands still tremble when I loosen the back of her dress. Eight weeks' absence is a long time to a soldier. I turned her face full to mine, that face so maddening in its self-containment. "You're being rough," she said. But I was not. I was being tender. I kissed her eyes, cheeks, lips with a frenzied tenderness, and slipped the dress down her shoulders. Above the corslet covering her breasts, and beneath her neck, a white landscape begins. This is her miracle. The skin seems almost luminous and is faintly patinated by trickling veins of blue. A little shadowed triangle dips between each shoulder under the long, silken ridge of the collar-bone. And somewhere beneath, before the real curve of the breasts begin, they are predicted by a faint, intimate lifting of soft flesh.

I know I'm an intemperate man, and although the murmurings of slaves and orderlies could be heard in the surrounding rooms, my words stumbled in worship and my kisses spread from her lips and neck down to this blessed landscape of her breast. But when I looked up I saw on her face that mute alarm which brings down a curtain between us. My lips were still pressed to her, but seemed colder now. She fondled my hair distantly, then said: "Will you have Maxi killed?"

I said: "Yes."

She asked: "Why? Isn't one enough?"

I asked her what she meant.

She said hesitantly: "My father."

I straightened in front of her. She made an unfinished gesture at pulling the dress over her shoulders. She looked apologetic. I felt confused, bitter. The passion had drained out of me. I said: "You know I wasn't responsible for his death. So why do you say this?" My voice sounded heckling. "He provoked a war I never wanted. I defeated and pardoned him. He hanged himself. In every way he was answerable for his own end. How could I stop it? In my opinion he was lucky. A man's lucky to die when and how he wants."

"Don't talk so loud." She was smiling now, this exasperating woman. "The eunuchs eavesdrop."

I said moodily: "I shout because you call me a murderer."

She pulled my head down to her breast and caressed it. She seemed sorry for me, almost condescending. She twisted my curls in her fingers.

For a little while I refused to kiss her. But then I again opened my lips against that warm silk of skin, while she remained standing above me, mocking, playing, laughing a little.

Sometimes I hate her.

For a few minutes we stayed like this. Then she stepped back from me, dressed herself and said in a voice of excitement: "Will you show me the siege-works?"

I said she couldn't go near. The enemy ballistas had sometimes thrown arrows eight hundred yards. But she tugged at my arm, smiling with feigned imperiousness, and cried: "Show me the siege-works, my Augustus!"

That is how the Empress came to Verona.

XII

*Bishop Hosius of Cordoba, to the Consecrated
Virgin Emilia, his sister, at Cordoba.*

[Undated]

OUR siege presses on very hard, dearest sister, as if we must suffocate this great city. But the reports are everywhere of an army marching against us from the east, so that the court camp has moved inside the military lines between huge earth ramparts, one facing Verona, the other facing out. We are forbidden to approach the front siege-works. But even if I could, I would spare you a description of such evil. All day I achieve nothing. The secretariats here have been thrown into confusion and the affairs of the faithful in Gaul, even the loudest petitions, do not occupy the minds of men who feel they may never see Gaul again.

In the middle of this danger the Empress has arrived from Milan. You will forgive me when I say that the presence of women in the army can only distract and inflame the senses of the men. The Empress herself, daughter of the persecutor, is a remarkably handsome woman, dazzling even, and her dress is modest. She has the white complexion which our Spanish ladies so much envy. But in her train are female servants and slaves, such as cause men to sin in their dreams. These are all a viper and a corruption of the spirit. The Empress's companion and her

39

wardrobe mistress are carried in litters about the camp. I have
witnessed such creatures before, whose beauty fatally impairs
them. Their energies are consumed in self-tenderness. In old age
they are grotesque.

How wisely was it said in the *Revelation* that those not defiled
with women would have the name of God written on their
foreheads! You, my dear, have chosen the better part: to abase
the low passions of the body, and to submit yourself to your Lord
in heaven rather than to any lord on earth. *That* Bridegroom will
never fail you.

[*Here follows an elucidation of the teaching of St. Paul on celibacy.*]

I believe that men and women are secretly repelled by their
own carnal affections. It must be so. Today I chanced to talk
briefly to the Augustus himself, whose wife has so recently
arrived. I mentioned our tradition: that *love covers many sins*. He
looked at me in a most strange way, and did not answer.

He is often frightening. He glares at one. The soldiers say that
his eyes resemble those of a lion. I have no idea about this.
Staring at a lion from close range is something an elderly man
can be pardoned for giving up. But I've noticed that the more
bellicose the Augustus is about a matter, the less he is sure.
Today he muttered that the gods of the underworld seemed to
have power on earth. His look demanded a reply.

"Fallen angels there may be," I said respectfully, "but in our
belief, Augustus, these other gods are dead."

This man is like a child sometimes. He said: "Are they? Are
they? What do your books say?"

"They say there is only One God, Augustus. One."

He seemed reassured by this answer.

I thank you for the solace of your letter, my sister, but cannot
tell, after all these years, when I may see you again. I think of you
often in Cordoba, and wonder: do our father's old ships still take
the iron down the river to Gades? Strange, the pictures one
conjures. Farewell, beloved Emilia. May God guard you.

XIII

*The Empress Fausta to her cousin Marina
at Nice.*

Verona, 4 September

HAVE you ever heard an army trumpet? They stand high as a man, are shaped as elongated lilies and sound like the bellowing of a bull. Imagine thirty of these lifted in the sun as Gaius arrived to greet me yesterday, while the sacred retinue fell on its face in the dust. How I love the army!

But Gaius looked gaunt. His mind is not only filled with the siege but is black with its own thoughts, and I find it hard to help him. Soon after our arrival he escorted Livilla and me to look at the siege-works. Livilla gives herself airs. I'm no judge, but I suspect she has no right. Her family owns sheep-farms and she smears her face in lycium, which makes her look as if she had jaundice. She was amused, at a distance, by the soldiers. She is used to the horsetail crests of the Italian legions and she thought our worn plumes a great joke, calling them donkey-hair. But when we came closer she turned quiet. Because these are not only handsome men, but purposeful and unpampered. What is more frightening than disciplined barbarism? At the same time they are oddly fastidious. They clean their armour with little bags of sand, and every evening their camps are hung thick with washing.

I wonder if you ever saw Verona? Such a beautiful city, Marina. The apartment houses show above the walls, with troughs of flowers suspended from the windows. Nothing has changed since my childhood, when we used to pass through on our way to Aquileia. Today, looking from our breastworks, I distinctly made out a woman on one of the balconies, watering her plants. So strange.

But at most parts of the walls the siege-engines are at work. You've never seen such monsters. Great catapults which they call 'wild asses' kick boulders at the city all day. Sometimes the legionaries rush battering-rams in wheeled sheds to the base of the walls; their roofs are covered in clay kneaded thick with hair so that the enemy's fire won't burn through. Gaius refused to let me watch this, but I saw several places where the stones had been smashed, then picked out with beams and hooks. The legions have now prepared wooden towers covered by hides. As soon as the ditches have been filled they plan to roll these against the ramparts and mount them. It's shamelessly exciting.

All along our palisades my husband leaves a ferment in his wake. Quietness pains him. Even I, who am used to him, was amazed by the rapidity of his orders, mostly given in an uncouth army Latin – almost another tongue. Soldiers' language bewilders me. They are always forming tortoise, or loading scorpions, or marching in serpent; you'd think they owned a zoo.

In the evening the commanders presented themselves. Even those I knew were so sunburnt that they looked quite changed. Tetricus, the praetorian prefect, is my husband's right arm – and a very heavy and vigorous one he is, a native Belgian. He was five years on the Rhine with Gaius, and before that in Africa and Syria, and before that fighting the Sarmatians on the Danube. He even marched with the Emperor Carus to Persia (he's a great bore on this) so he must be nearing fifty.

Then there's Sacrovir, the commander of the cavalry, a little fair-bearded Gaul, very truculent. His favourite sport, apparently, is tormenting the Chief Marshal, a ponderous Briton already worn to a skeleton by rough weather campaigning. Of the legionary prefects our favourite is the only Italian, Verinus, who is just like a boy. You can't imagine a man less scarred by war. He saved Gaius' life fighting against the Cherusci.

The last to appear at this reception was the chief of the German auxiliaries. Oh Marina, I had to put on the most ferocious face to stop myself laughing! All the other commanders have turned black as Nubians in the sun, but not him. He blundered over to me dressed in woollen leggings – an enormous man. His skin had been burnt to a most vivid and terrible pink and his red hair burst up from his head in flames. Just like a sunrise.

Ah – I've forgotten one other general. And that's the source of his strength: he evades notice – Geta, Master of the Offices and head of the secret police. This is a Dacian, dark, slight, almost insignificant-looking. He smiles diffidently, good-naturedly all the time. I believe he is merciless.

Gaius trusts all these men and seems to know their limits. But he has another retainer who trusts none of them, and even has the insolence to scowl at *me*. Always on campaign my husband is

42

followed about by this old Illyrian servant Cecrops, an ex-slave, an ex-soldier, an ex-human, who has all the arrogance and snobbery of the imperial chattel. He has served Gaius since childhood. He tastes his food, bears his armour and insists on sleeping against his door, to the chagrin of the imperial body-guard. He also trims the Eternal beard every morning, since he is the only man Gaius allows near his throat with a razor. Need I say it? I hate him.

You tell me, dear cousin, that I want to be married to a myth, not to a man. Well, Gaius is already a legend to his soldiers and a god to his subjects. But to himself he is a mystery. When I arrived here I found him nervous and brooding. He left the siege for an hour and escorted me to my quarters, where I gave him some small gifts. His gratitude was painful. I suddenly noticed how helpless and frustrated he looked, with his great haggard body sitting upright in a chair, as if he had still to play the god-emperor. The campaign has been fast and difficult, I know. But he looks as he does (and I whisper this to you) because he's no longer sure if the sun shines on him. He's afraid of being abandoned. I don't know why this is. The sun to me is as bright as it ever was. But then I do not feel as he does. Gaius always had to sense the rush of divine life through him. That has made him what he is.

Now suddenly it's gone. How terrible that must be, Marina, as if the earth moved from under you! He suspects he may have lost the God's favour somehow, and done wrong – and his con-fusion is terrible. Am I explaining it at all? Probably not. These troubles seem beyond my reach. I wonder why. It's as if he talked of colours which I cannot see. I can only watch his struggle with a kind of awe. While he wrestles with divine powers, I am bossing my seamstress.

But there's one source of his anxiety still more frightening to write about: my brother Maxentius. He's gone to the limits to damn us, and I cannot describe to you with what a sense of fear, irritation and betrayal I listened to what he'd done. I hear you ask, why irritation? That's because Gaius is so bull-headed sometimes. Really, Marina, I ask myself: how did such a stupid man become Augustus of Gaul and Britain? Oh how precariously the world is run! One moment this man is supreme. The next, I think my serving-girl knows more than he does. He can no more guess a man like Maxi than he can see in pitch darkness. He imagines everybody to be bound in the same net of conscience as himself. It's terrifying. Compared to my brother he's an infant.

As for my fear, it is rooted in childhood memories. And my feeling of betrayal too. I, you see, was my brother's familiar. And all the time that Gaius was talking – with the puzzled outrage of somebody glimpsing a hell he cannot comprehend – I was feeling: that's my brother, I remember that, that's us.

Imagine two children – a brute-faced boy and a skinny girl – squatting in a portico at night. For all I know, my innocent cousin, you were with us in Milan that year, but you would have been in bed. We held a slate which we had driven through with pins. I remember Maxi's face like a weird dog's in the moonlight. On one side of the slate he had inscribed the symbol of Hecate, goddess of infernal regions; on the other side the boat of Charon sailing on the night waters. We were going to kill our tutor. I was trembling all over, not with fear but with unearthly fascination and excitement. I believed absolutely in our power: we had spells to awake the whole demonic world. I shiver still at the laurel bushes along the edge of the courtyard, which glinted strangely, while stripes of moonlight fell through the colonnade. Everything was pregnant and waiting. And now Maxi scratched under the symbol of Hecate (I remember the words to this hour): 'We consecrate the tutor Milo, son of Alina. May he be eliminated from human sight. *Phrix, phrox*. May his bones be smashed and his heart withered.'

Just then the wind rose. It seemed like a sign. We tiptoed to the courtyard well. Maxi leant over and nailed the slate between its stones. Next he took a dead chameleon from his pouch, threw it in and recited: "Hecate closes out the light." Then we ran.

Our tutor lives robustly to this day, but my memory is sallow and corrupt with what we did. My childhood was full of such things.

Yet as for Gaius, I have faith that magic can't hurt him. I've told you this before, and can't explain it. Even when he feels deserted by the God, he seems closer to sanctity than I. I wish I could give him confidence. But I cannot give him anything he needs. God and passion are for finer souls than mine.

I'm sending you some Calabrian honey. I had jars and jars of it brought from Milan. One gets petty longings here.

XIV

Commonplace Book of Synesius, Master of the Sacred Memory and private secretary to Constantine.

6 September

MOSQUITOES intolerable. Whine, bite, whine, all night. We're downriver from the legions here, and the water sends up noxious smells. The whole river has become a Gallic lavatory. And people say a soldier's life is healthy.

Every evening, when I enter the Augustus' quarters, Cecrops jumps at me from his hiding-place and demands my name. My nerves are thinning, along with everyone else's. These days the Augustus dismisses me earlier than he did, and I lie in the dark listening to whine, bite, whine, together with the ceaseless pacing of his feet across the neighbouring room. Then comes the squeal of his stylus preparing the everlasting orders, letters, plans – and finally memoirs, like a mendicant scrap-dealer sorting out the jumble of his mind. I reflect with astonishment that for more than forty years the Roman Empire has been ruled by a succession of Illyrian peasants, unversed in either art or science.

The news is now that the relieving army of Pompeianus is less than twenty miles away, and that tomorrow we shall fight. All around, the hammering of armourers and the rasp of sharpening swords fills me with misery, not because of what the swords will do, but because it stops me sleeping. I'm reduced to an animal. With every breath I must be drinking in brutality, but I've got used to it.

Ever since we moved inside the earthworks, my secretariat has been pandemonium. Today the notaries were surreptitiously packing up again, ready to march south or flee north. If we enter Rome alive, I'll sacrifice to Janus. Our tents are so jumbled in with those of the consistory and the Bishop of Cordoba that we receive each other's memoranda. Thus I am exposed to visits from the bishop, a fat, twinkling man fond of talking about the transfiguring power of Christ. I tell him I've seen a good many of these fellows who've 'put on the new man created after the likeness of God', as they say, and they cheat and stink like the old ones. Perhaps this will end our association.

45

Three days ago the Empress arrived and our camp was agreeably infused by young slave girls. The Augustus, I hear, escorted her about the siege-works, leaving out the nastier bits. I was struck again by the appearance of this woman – fruit of a mercenary marriage and a loveless childhood. I find her chilling, though many admire her. She looks like a leopardess baffled in mid-leap. Even the eyes are not soft, but lustrous and slightly aggressive. She will support Constantine against her brother without remorse, just as she supported him against her father. The Augustus is probably the only man for whom she has any feelings, and I am not even sure of the nature of these. Together they generate an extraordinary intensity. You cannot tell whether they are about to clasp one another's hands or tear each other's faces. Perhaps he still loves her.

This evening I walked along our lines, maybe for the last time. Verona remains untaken, and I think of Hannibal, who failed in Italy because he could not capture cities. Recently archers from the walls have been firing messages into our breastworks, telling the soldiers that the barbarians have crossed the Rhine and are ravaging their women. The enemy must have a high opinion of our army's literacy. The regular legionaries have used the messages for cleaning out their nostrils. As for the German auxiliaries, they are probably the barbarians the enemy has in mind. Tonight I witnessed their ritual before battle. They were whispering to their spears in the moonlight, caressing the shafts as if they were lovers.

The Augustus and the praetorian prefect rode along the lines all evening, talking to the tribunes. The men cheered them rapturously and followed them with torches, touching their clothes and harness. Later the Chief Marshal arrived, issuing directives for tomorrow. Tomorrow, tomorrow! They look forward to it as to a carnival!

I find myself asking the question which no soldier dares ask on the night of battle. What if we lose? A Rhineland army in Italy has no escape, and will not be forgiven. 'In war one may' not blunder twice.' If I survive interrogation by the tyrant's police, I dare say I shall be given a quiet job somewhere. Lucky Synesius! I'll become responsible for the drainage in Modena, or be clerk to a provincial tax-collector. Then perhaps I'll find time for completing my *Some Aspects of Reason in Epicurus*.

Or will I end my days entering figures in columns? It's good to foresee this and write it down: the imagined never happens.

I extinguish the lamp. Whine, bite. Every two hours I have to get up, because my bladder has weakened. Noble thoughts on the eve of conflict.

XV

The Empress Fausta to Tetricus, Praetorian Prefect.

Evening, 6 September

I BEG you to restrain my husband from any rash action tomorrow. He too easily exposes himself. Have a mind to this. Should he suffer any hurt, he may forgive you, but I shall not. May the gods give victory.

XVI

The Empress Fausta to her cousin Marina at Nice.

7 September

THIS letter will be delayed, since nothing is allowed out of our camp. But I must tell you now what has happened. More than thirty thousand men – almost three quarters of the army – marched west this morning to meet the forces of Pompeianus. Since then, silence.

Gaius crossed the river before dawn to ready the troops on the far side. In the early morning he returned, surrounded by his bodyguard, and we set out, I in my carriage and he riding, for the level ground west of our ramparts. I've never seen such a sight as greeted us: the whole of the First Minervia and Eighth Augusta legions – twelve thousand men drawn up in battle array. And the sun just rising over Verona. It stopped my heart. The moment Gaius' purple cloak was seen a huge cry of 'Augustus!' went up, and was repeated over and over. He at once saluted the standards, raising his helmet so the men could see his face. Then we mounted a makeshift podium. My hand rested on his arm. Behind our chairs stood Tetricus, the praetorian prefect, and Sacrovir, commander of the cavalry, with the staff tribunes.

It was a heady moment. When Gaius ordered the standards advanced they came forward like a golden forest. Behind the imperial eagle I saw the goat emblem of my own Augusta legion, and behind that a glinting mass of gilded wreaths and wings, all the standards of the cohorts and the centuries. You've never seen such a sight, Marina, and the standard-bearers themselves, crowned by the heads of leopards and bears, looked like a host of animals walking upright.

When the generals advanced to the salute, the tribunes of the Augusta saluted me and their ranks suddenly broke into cheering. It sounded spontaneous and I think they're proud to see their Empress on the battlefield. I wonder when that last happened? Perhaps your Lucullus will know. What they really thought of me I cannot guess. But I was wearing a Sidonian purple embroidered in gold and I hope I looked like the Empress of Rome as well as of Gaul. Gaius says the Augusta is his finest legion, and one of the oldest in the Empire.

My memory becomes confused after this, although I recall that the priests sacrificed to the Sun and to Mars. Then Gaius stood up and addressed the men. He harangued them for four minutes, which he says is the longest a legionary can listen to anything but a ribald story. It was a wonderful display and I could see why the soldiers love him. He looked like the god they feel him to be: tall and powerful as a tree with all the craggy strength in his face lit up by the young sun. I've never felt so proud. I simply stared at him. He spoke in such a voice that more than half of those thousands must have heard him. But it was a very simple speech. He reminded them of their past valour and the campaigns they had fought together, then ridiculed the enemy with a coarse expression which set the nearest cohorts laughing. He held up Rome like a prize before their eyes, then conjured the winter Alps behind them to intimate the price of failure. Yes, in four minutes he played on their loyalty, their arrogance, their sense of humour, their tradition and their fear.

The moment he finished they clashed their shields against their armoured knees. I can't describe to you what that sounds like. Its clamour rolled in terrible waves back and forth over the whole army, and will roll like that in my nightmares.

But Gaius was smiling. He said: "That's their tribute." He ordered the Minervia to march. I saw Verinus salute us, with the legion's standard behind him. The next moment Gaius had embraced me gravely, and stepped down from the dais. It was only then that I realised he was going. I followed him to his horse, my dignity gone. I don't know what I meant to say. His helmet always transforms him. I was tongue-tied. He mounted and muttered to me: "The commander of your bodyguard has orders not to let you move beyond camp. Don't embarrass him by trying."

I kissed his hand. And now he is gone.

Later

It's night. A messenger has just arrived to say that at dusk the battle was still raging. He said it was impossible to tell who had gained ground. But he thought our own men were outnumbered. That is all I know.

I write this on the rooftop of my villa. Sometimes I think I hear a sound like faint, continuous cymbals in the distance. But I may be imagining it, or the sound may be quite close. Livilla says she cannot hear it at all, nor can that waspish old Synesius who's sitting with us. It's absurd how quickened my senses have become. I'm now familiar with a thousand minute noises. I could hear an ant breathe.

Verona itself is silent. The torches on our earthworks ring the whole city in fire. The remains of our legions are quiet too. The feeling of waiting is unbearable. The only activity is that of priests. They have not stopped sacrificing since morning and the night is full of incense. Just now I went downstairs to find my servants packing my clothes and papers. I've never been so furious, and I think they are now more frightened of me than of the battle. But I sense that the whole court camp is secretly preparing for flight. So I've left my horses unharnessed and conspicuous at tether in front of the villa, with the carriages idle.

And so we wait. Those disembodied cymbals are still sounding out there in the dark. I'm not exactly afraid. At least I don't think this is fear. My hand is steady, isn't it? I'll draw you a circle. [She does so.] You see.

But calmness would be easier if my servant girls stopped weeping. Livilla keeps trembling too, and cries at every noise. "Oh! What's that?" While I only think it.

Synesius says the state papers in his charge are all in one tent and that he has a barrel of pitch sufficient to fire them, together with those of the consistory. I warm to him. He doesn't seem afraid. But he keeps going to the lavatory.

I occupy myself with reading your last letter. You say the world has changed too much, and that you are afraid to bring children into it. What nonsense! We, and the world they find, will equip them. So don't worry about the children. Worry about yourself. At twenty-five, dear Marina, you must be getting old.

Apparently another messenger has reached the siege-works. He was covered in blood, but it wasn't his own. I'm sending a servant to find out the news.

XVII

Journal-Memoir of Constantine.

7 September

BY noon we had left the river and were marching across open country. A detachment of cavalry had sighted the enemy advancing along the axis of the Aquileia road. We moved forward in a flexible formation: the two full legions in the centre, cohorts supporting and the cavalry easing round our flanks. After days of siege the mobility of the legions in the flatlands was a relief. There was little to disturb the uniformity of this country: a group of orchards, a faint swell of hill on our left. It was a cavalry commander's dream. The Sun burnt bright but not hot, and would soon fall behind us to shine in the enemy's eyes. The glow and the mild warmth of Him suffused me. It was a good omen. My mind felt vigorous but calm. Beside me Tetricus grumbled about the size of the enemy forces, and it was certain now that we were heavily outnumbered. But I have heard that grumbling often and know it as a safeguard against carelessness.

Towards mid-afternoon the enemy forces materialised out of the distance. At first it was hard to tell their composition, because they shone in a shadowless ray of steel across the whole horizon. But they were advancing fast and their pattern quickly became clear. They dangerously outflanked us. Pompeianus obviously planned to compass us by superior numbers before we had time to widen our front. We halted. I advanced our standards at once. The centre legions stood firm and I ordered the cohorts of the Primigenia and Ulpia Victrix thinned and extended, while the cavalry deployed farther out. It was done as precisely as if on exercise although the enemy was now less than six hundred yards from us.

Within minutes our forces would lock. Tetricus and I studied their advance without speaking. Every battle I've fought has been won in these few, hesitant minutes before a javelin has been thrown. At this time the threats and weaknesses of the enemy are clear, while mobility is still possible. Such moments have a nervous, pregnant quality even for the men. They are the worst, and the most decisive, of battle.

The threat came from the centre. We recognised it at once. Even behind a screen of spearmen the scale armour of heavy Sarmatian cavalry emits a peculiar glint. The endangered legion was the Eighth Augusta. I remembered the lessons of my past – Persia, Moesia, Turin – and loosened the legion into open order. Under cover of the front ranks the clubmen of the Minervia thickened the Augusta's rear. The whole body was now absorbent as a sponge.

Three hundred yards. The enemy standards shone clear. In front of the Sarmatians marched a screen of Sicilian foot. Very full Italian legions moved on either side: Tuscan for the most part, with heavy groupings of cohorts flanking them, whose standards were indistinguishable to me. Far to our left their cavalry was concealed by dust; to our right a cloud of light Mauretanian horse covered the fields. We were outnumbered perhaps five to three.

I never commit men to battle without a pang at the moment of impact. The imperial legion is the most perfect weapon in the world, and a general may well watch it with pride as he watches his horses in a chariot-race. But always at this time, for a sinking second, I remember standing myself in the front line against a Persian onslaught, where I was placed as a raw tribune by the Caesar Galerius, in his hope that I'd be killed. The feelings and sensations of that time – the smell of sweat and garlic, the sense of dependence on the man to either side, the tension of the throwing-arm poised under its javelin, the calculation of paces – all touch me still with respect and anxiety for these veterans.

That moment was now on us. The enemy was fifty yards away. They were advancing in the stylised march of Sparta – two paces, an ominous pause, two paces. Then they charged.

The shock of our javelins stopped the front rank. It succumbed into the second. Only Sarmatian armour can halt a javelin flung at ten paces. Then we were committed hand-to-hand, and the noise was terrible and simultaneous all along our centre.

Tetricus said: "This is going to outlast the daylight." Already our shadows lay long on the grass.

To our right four cohorts of the Ulpia Victrix were stationed on the edge of olive orchards. I withdrew their front into the trees to break up the attacks of the Moorish cavalry, then sent orders to Sacrovir. While a screen of legionary horses sent up curtains of dust on the flank of the Victrix, I had him transfer the weight of his cavalry to our left flank. Here, where the ground lifted a little, I meant to turn the enemy and cut into the heavy Tuscan legions.

The Sicilian troops had disintegrated and scattered from the Augusta. But there was no significance in this. Pompeianus had planned it. And now, riding over the welter of Sicilian dead and wounded, the Sarmatians charged in a body so compact that even where we stood the ground vibrated. Men and horses were covered with a scale armour whose strength no sword can pierce. They crashed through our front ranks and plunged heavily into the loose, absorbent mass of the legion. We knew this was a crisis. I rode my staff close against our rear. The distinctive wedge of conical helmets was pressing in deeper and deeper. Nothing seemed to stop it. We could now separate the individuals from the mass, less like men than great silver reptiles. So close did they come to breaking through that I could make out their wide-jawed serpent standards jostling not fifty paces away. Such men could only be clubbed to death. The scar which this charge left on the Augusta has yet to be effaced. But little by little its impact slowed and the unwieldy horsemen became clogged among the legionaries. Their armour's weight had sapped them. They moved almost dreamily now, with strange, bovine turnings of their heads. The clubmen did terrible execution. Some of these mailed giants had to be flailed twenty times over before they fell dead or unconscious, and their harness slit open with daggers. Their huge horses, moving as if blind, escaped riderless into the country behind us.

The entire army was now engaged hand-to-hand. The exhaustion of the Augusta and the thinness of our whole right flank exposed the Minervia to the weight of the Italian legions. But their wing was covered by the Ulpia Victrix, who maintained an obstinate stand among the orchards, surrounded by a tempest of Mauretanian cavalry. On our left, where Sacrovir's horsemen were cutting a deep swathe, the enemy was beginning to fall back.

There now occurred one of those pointless and wasteful incidents with which every general is familiar. For some time a small cloud of dust had been gathering behind us, and I detached some men to reconnoitre. They returned to report the approach of three hundred Frankish auxiliary horse, whom I had posted at the ford under one of their petty chieftains. I ordered this force to return at once, but the chieftain, who was drunk, rode up and hurled himself at my feet, imploring to be permitted to fight. When I again ordered him back he remounted and made as if to obey. Then suddenly he wheeled his men about, led them to our right and charged the Mauretanian cavalry. These are Moorish light horsemen, very agile. Their technique with the javelin is perfectly adapted to the charge of loosely-disciplined lancers. Within minutes they had surrounded the Franks and slaughtered them to a man.

By now the Minervia was falling back. The press of the Italian legions was terrible on them. But they retreated with deliberation, taking their toll. I told Tetricus to bolster them, although all I could give him was a handful of my guard.

He said: "You must not stay unprotected, Augustus."

It sounded peculiarly like an order. I commanded him to go.

At this time, in spite of our peril, I thought that the battle lay in our favour. Our right wing was almost holding, our centre was relieved of the Sarmatians, and on the left Sacrovir's cavalry threatened to turn the first Tuscan legion. My staff looked steady, and the younger aides excited. I felt a familiar exultance through my body. This rich and incomprehensible feeling surged in my muscles and filled my chest like a wineskin. If it had a voice, it said: 'You are invulnerable. You are going to conquer.' I looked at the Sun behind us. He hung in a mistless orb, golden and friendly. Once again that Presence was mine, the Sun Invincible. I cannot have noticed how low He had fallen in the sky.

I stationed myself on the flank of the Minervia, well forward, to encourage them. Verinus joined me, pouring sweat but unhurt. The rear ranks shouted my name. Their javelins were expended and the dinning of swords on shields made a harsh, long roar all along the line. Against us the Italians were flexible and clever. But my own men, taller, struck with the hard, disciplined strokes of seasoned backs and arms, and even in retreat preserved an impenetrable rampart of iron.

Verinus seized my wrist. "If you want us to stand we'll stand, Gaius."

I said: "No. Retreat slowly. Save casualties. We're destroying their left."

Now a curious moment. I think I saw Pompeianus. I was looking across to the standard of the enemy legion. Beneath it, with the prefect, stood a grizzled man in a scarlet cloak. I am sure it was him. I could almost make out his expression. When I was a youth we'd campaigned together in Diocletian's expedition against Egypt, and he'd patiently explained to me the siege of Alexandria.

Verinus was shouting in my ear: "What's happened to the Victrix?"

I said: "They'll hold." But in fact I was growing worried. The few cavalry left on that flank could only feint at the Mauretanians, and the Victrix were slowly contracting into the trees, leaving behind their dead. Opposite us now a sickly pink light gilded the Italians as they advanced. I glanced behind me to see the Sun almost descended. An ache and an irrational hollowness sounded in me. I withdrew from the Minervia. The Chief Marshal reported that on one side Sacrovir's cavalry and the Primigenia were rolling back the Tuscans; but that on the other the enemy were close to breaking through. A breach had opened between the Minervia and the Victrix, filled only by dead.

With a chilling heart I ordered the line of the Minervia to be thinned and extended. As suddenly as the Sun had granted me confidence, so now an inexplicable foreboding was spreading in me. Tetricus arrived with one hand soaked in blood. He looked grim. He wanted the Victrix withdrawn. It was tantamount to ordering a full retreat, and the Moors would have harassed them cruelly. I refused.

My aides had fallen quiet; and now my presentiment was heightened by a trivial happening. In battle you may see a hundred men die and forget all but one. This man you will remember for ever. I was close behind the last rank of the Minervia when a young centurion stumbled towards me holding out his hands. I had the foolish idea that he wanted to give me something. But when he reached my horse he touched the hem of my robe with his fingers, pensively almost, and gazed at me with a most pitiful worship. I reached down to him and saw a hilt protruding from his stomach. He refused to take my hand. The next moment the blood sprang from his mouth and my aides were kicking away the corpse.

I sat rigid on my horse. By now, such was our pressure on the left and the enemy's on our right that the whole field of battle threatened to swing round west to north. But the course of it was sliding beyond my grasp. I told myself: 'The fall of the Sun is not a sign; the earth is interposed in His way. That is all.' But I understand when men say that the virtue has gone out of them. It had happened to me before, although never as now. Behind me the Sun set in a pitiless fire. He seemed to go down with purpose, portending my failure. But what was my sin? My expression as I watched Him must have been openly bitter because the Marshal said: "You can't help the night, Augustus." I turned back to the battlefield with a sense of desolation. In the dimness obscure masses of men were struggling together for a reason I'd almost forgotten. My staff looked jaded and impotent. I noticed the sweat on the back of my hands and their stiffness, clutching the reins. Why was I turned into a child? I looked back. The last, shallow arc of light had fallen from sight. The God had gone.

I turned my back on Him. I had a feeling as if insects were creeping along my veins. Tetricus asked: "What's angered you?" I thought: am I angry? Then I noticed that I was. My head was on

55

fire. Yes, I was raging to pull the God back by the hair. I have heard of men gnashing their teeth before, but I had never done it until now. I drew my sword.

Tetricus put a hand on my rein. "I think we should still wait, Augustus."

I said: "We're useless here. In a moment it'll be night. We must encourage the Victrix while they can still see who we are." While all the time I was saying to myself, or to the God: I'm not a child. I'm not powerless. I have a will and power of my own.

I galloped to our right without looking behind me, knowing my staff and remaining guard must follow. We were barely a hundred men. Already a few Mauretanian cavalry had trickled through our lines and were hovering on the rear of the Victrix, afraid to attack alone. We drove them off. Among the trees the four cohorts were bent in a deep arc, their shields clamped together, fending off Moorish spears on one side and Italian infantry on the other.

I now did something for which later I was censured by leaders of my staff – not for exposing them but for exposing myself. If unsatisfied, my anger could carry me to the edge of the world; but a single violent act thins it to air. And now I did not lead these men within the protective arc of the cohorts, but a little to the left. Our approach was concealed by dusk and the olive trees and we hit the Italian infantry at an angle. For a moment they must have thought themselves seriously assailed. A legionary with a broken shield was the first in my way. He did not even see me until my horse's head was level with him and my sword-arm falling. My guards cut down some twenty men, with a centurion and one of the standards of the centuries. Tetricus was so concerned with edging me out of danger that he almost lost his horse. We veered back towards the Victrix.

The moment my sword had struck, a calm descended on me. I do not understand myself any more than my commanders do. And it's typical of war that these cohorts, who to us seemed so imperilled, were surprised at our concern for them. Their tribunes were untroubled. They despised the Moors and outnumbered the Italians.

Dislocated, Tetricus and I rested among the rough, quiet trunks of the olive trees while the Marshal moved about with our few cavalry, telling the cohorts that their Emperor was here.

Tetricus looked at me. We suddenly burst out laughing. "Rest a few minutes," I said. "It's a soldiers' battle now."

[*From the Report of the Chief Marshal to the Sacred Historian:* Seeing that the Sun was declining, and realising that by night he would be unable to give his divine succour and direction to the troops, a great anger at the enemy fell on our beloved Emperor. It has been inferred by some wicked persons that the Emperor was angry with the Sun Himself for setting while the issue of the field was yet doubtful. This is not so for I, his unworthy servant and Marshal, was present. It was now with high audacity that the Augustus attacked the enemy and made a great slaughter to aid the cohorts of the Victrix. . . .]

[*From the Commonplace Book of Synesius:* I spoke to the praetorian prefect about the part played early in the battle by Constantine. He said that every decision which the Augustus made by daylight had been masterly. But towards sunset the Emperor began glancing at the sky. Tetricus knew what this meant. In times of heightened anxiety the Augustus becomes sensitive to every sign. The sun, he now said, was setting 'on purpose'. At that moment a centurion of the Minervia, who had been stabbed in the belly, blundered over with his last breath and lifted his eyes to the Augustus as to a god. The moment he looked at him, he died. The prefect suspected that this had filled Constantine with a sense of helplessness, or even of hypocrisy. But no sooner had the sun set than a change came over him and his features were transformed by the most bitter rage. Tetricus has known Constantine many years and told me he thought that this was not truly anger with the God, but anger with himself.

I'm sure that the prefect is right. I suspect that dependence on the God reduces Constantine to slavery, and that for this he cannot forgive himself. Like a child, he is angry at his own powerlessness. Because for Constantine power is truth. In other words, he himself wishes to be the God.]

The night was upon us. A light wind sprang up, and a half moon appeared in the sky. The battlefield no longer yielded patterns and currents, but was reduced to a darkened sea of struggling men, who could glimpse no more than the man opposite. The issue now belonged to them, not to us. Briefly I covered one flank of the Victrix with my guard – no longer an emperor but a squadron commander. The Moors had spent their javelins and now made desultory attacks through the orchards. They were too light to dent the cohorts, but they were hard to trap. Riding bareback behind small round shields, they charged suddenly out of darkness, and as suddenly vanished. Twice we galloped in pursuit only to lose them among the glades of moonlight between trees. These became a maze distinguished from one another only by the attitudes of their dead: a stiffened Moor in one; and in another a cavalry decurion whose helmet, caught in the branches where he dangled, had choked him with its strap.

This dealing with phantoms continued far into the night and along our whole front, where we tried to encourage prefects who could scarcely see us, to locate units which had vanished, and sent messengers who never returned. At other times, conscious of our futility, I would rein in my staff and momentarily listen, with helpless tension, to the invisible clashing and groaning.

Standing unrecognised in the lines of the Primigenia we glimpsed other things which a commander doesn't witness. An impatient trooper in the second rank plucked off the skull plate of a dead man's helmet, urinated into it and hurled it at the enemy. Nearby a cohort's standard was being tugged between a fat-faced enemy trooper and the bearer, who was growling under his leopardskin headdress as if pretending to be a real leopard in the dark. So they tugged and jostled in the middle of death, like two bad-tempered children. In another part of the field we were passed by one of Sacrovir's cavalry commanders, his lower jaw sheared away, gesticulating orders to his men.

It must have been after midnight that a gradual change came over the field. For a long time I had sensed a desperation in the enemy's pressing us. Their dead began to show thick on the grass behind our legions, many already stiffened. We were advancing. To our left the sound of fighting had travelled far ahead of us, and now dimmed. In the centre, soldiers of the Augusta were haphazardly supporting the Minervia. They too must have advanced, because now the scaly corpses of the Sarmatians became visible behind them, like stranded fish. For several hours small enemy reinforcements had been appearing piecemeal from the east. These now stopped. Over half the battlefield the enemy formations were breaking up. We could dimly see the massed gleam of their helmets loosening and diffusing into the darkness behind them, where Sacrovir's cavalry was ranging at will.

The battle was won.

Synesius says that the mind has many rooms, and at this moment my own was filled with pride, relief and bewilderment. But confusion at the God's inscrutability was submerged by sadness. I've fought thirteen heavy battles before, all against orientals and barbarians. But now, when dawn shone over the field, I saw little but slaughtered Romans, friend and foe alike, as if I'd attacked some elemental force which had ravaged us and left behind no dead of its own. The body of Pompeianus, unrecognisable but for his scarlet cloak, was brought to me in triumph. He was killed late in the night by men of the Augusta. I could not be glad.

Night battles bring their own waste. A signifer of the Ulpia Victrix, a giant of a man, was found dead with his javelin through one of his own legionaries. And it appears that our own cavalry attacked the first cohort of the Primigenia, killing its tribune.

I rode over the field with Tetricus. It's a commonplace among generals that there's much to be learnt from inspecting the aftermath of a battle. In my experience the field is generally a greater muddle than the battle was, and one mainly learns numbness. I found Verinus being carried off with a spear-wound in the hip. He grinned at me, said it was slight. Another casualty was Anulinus [a tribune?] whose death went unnoticed until this morning.

Wherever we turned were the dead. Their numbers exceeded those of any of my battles. Many of the enemy looked like fresh recruits. I noticed at least two who had fruitlessly cut off their thumbs to avoid conscription. This afternoon Tetricus produced a provisional casualty list. We have lost seven tribunes, thirty-two centurions and over three thousand men. The enemy lost four times that number.

If the God is not with me, I've become a Nero.

XVIII

Commonplace Book of Synesius.

THIS afternoon I visited the battlefield with the imperial physician. The Gallic legionaries were stripping armour from the fallen enemy, and complaining that it was too small for them. And certainly there could be no greater contrast than that between the Gaul and the Italian. These dead Tuscans and Romans appeared flaccid beside our men. Once their armour was off, their sternness was gone. The bodies looked tender and the faces, resting in their blood, showed female lashes and lips.

Even the physician, who is used to such sights, was shocked by the numbers of the fallen. As for me, never before have I seen a battlefield. The strange and pitiful thing is that the slain no longer seem to hate one another. They lie all together, their hands and limbs touching. The gulf which once existed between two armies now lies instead between the living and the dead. Each repudiates the other. It made me guilty to look at them.

XIX

Journal-Memoir of Constantine.

8 September

VERONA has surrendered.

My joy was tempered by utter physical weariness after battle. I had not slept for thirty-five hours and could hardly sit my horse while the city prefect read a dignified speech, and the gates were opened. By my side the heavy, scarred head of Tetricus kept dropping onto his armoured chest. I ordered in four fresh cohorts, handed over the city's administration to the Master of the Offices, retired to my quarters and fell asleep in full armour.

Towards evening, surrounded by the unnatural silence of a sleeping camp, I woke to find myself in bed where servants had carried my August Presence without its waking up. Ignominy!

I sent a message to Fausta, telling her I'd join her after the first watch. Downstairs, groups of officials were waiting for me in moods of pride and jubilation. The number of our prisoners is so great that I sent orders for them to be herded into the amphitheatre, where their manacles are still being beaten out from the metal of their swords. The battlefield I have left to the Marshal. It lies more than ten miles distant, but I am sure that this evening the air was tinged with the smell of cremations.

By the twelfth hour I had devolved command. I bathed and oiled myself and felt my muscles relax at last into a firm glow. The violence in my mind had been exorcised by success. I felt pleasure, touched with vanity. I say I hate flattery and that it creates self-deceit. Yet the adulation of my visitors, their petty panegyrics and hand-kissings, pleased me greatly. Only an elderly Veronese ex-senator, seeking permission to recover the body of his slain son, looked at me with pure hatred. This annoyed me so much that I almost refused him. Constantine, beware.

I rode to the court camp with a torchbearer. It was now late, and Fausta had dismissed her servants. She was waiting for me alone in the villa's reception room, her face burning with triumph. The moment I entered she cried in a strange blend of excitement and formality: "Victor! Victor! Victor!" She laid her hands on my shoulders and kissed my cheeks with imperious respect. For a whole hour I had to fight the battle again, reclining on a couch, while she lay beside me and tried to clarify advances and retreats by indenting patterns with her fingernails on a silk cushion. How had her Augusta legion fought? Good. But she was not sure if I should have exposed the Ulpia Victrix like that. Couldn't the legionary cavalry have cut up the Moors before transferring to the left wing? Oh. Why were Moors so difficult to catch? So I was right after all. Mauretanian horses. How had I known what to do about Sarmatian cavalry? And all the time her eyes were glittering with the animation of our victory.

She shows a grasp of tactics, but little of strategy. I told her I'd make her a centurion. "A hundred men!" she laughed. "One is too much for me!" The next moment she was asking about the surrender of Verona.

I told her that within three days we'd be marching on Aquileia; after that, south. I reminded her that if she remained she'd be a temptation to any determined local commander wanting to return Maxentius his sister. She must either come with us, or go back to Turin.

"No, I won't go back to Turin," she said. "I'd be bored. I'm coming with you."

"You speak as if it was a litter-ride to the sea." But her determination is quite familiar to me. I used to tell her it inhabited the space between her eyes, where a small, resolute knot sometimes gathers.

"We'll enter Rome together," she said. "All the way to the Palatine!"

"Yes," I said. "You will lead. The Lady Politta will follow. I, with a few others, will supply the rear. Not since . . ."

"The Lady Politta is sick," Fausta interrupted. "She thinks she's got dysentery. She says it's spreading in the army."

"My men don't have dysentery," I said. "They can eat anything and survive, like Arabian ostriches. How is it all your companions sicken? Do you cook for them? . . ."

For a while we bantered in a way we had not done for months. I wondered why we couldn't usually be like this. Am I too serious? Or is she? Almost always we create a tension together. We're wary of one another, like wounded gladiators. Perhaps I am as much a mystery and an ambiguity to her as she is to me – or as I to myself. Even my soldiers, I'm told, lampoon me in muddled ways: as child and veteran, prude and sensualist, master of earth and slave of heaven. But they at least love me.

Fausta had taken the jewelled circlet out of her hair and was setting it in mine. "I'm crowning you emperor," she said, "of Rome."

I stopped her. "Don't tempt the gods."

She was kneeling on the couch, looking down at me. "The emperor is among the gods."

I said: "That is very different."

Sometimes a tiny action of this woman ignites my desire and now, picking the circlet from my head in her long, sensitised fingers, she replaced it, with an odd caress, on her own. "One more battle," she said, "then your crowning will be true."

I kissed her lips. "You know nothing about it."

"Synesius says that . . ."

"Synesius also knows nothing about it." I got up from the couch, pulling her after me, and extinguished all the lamps but one, which I carried into the bedroom.

"But even Tetricus says Aquileia will surrender now." She climbed up to the bed alcove, started to take off her dress, then sat down on the valance. The isolation of her, framed in the half-lit recess, was irritating. I ascended beside her and pulled her dress to the floor. She sat upright on the bed, naked and laughing at me. "You have no confidence in the future, Gaius. It's I who have confidence."

I scarcely listened. I noticed the coarseness of my hands trembling over her skin, how thick and scarred they were — almost a defilement to her breasts. The lamp's light was weak at the other side of the room. It discovered all the intricacy of her body, picked out the strange, small gulfs of breast and shoulder which have mesmerised and maddened me so long.

"If you don't storm Aquileia we'll be wintering on the Adriatic. That would be insufferable." She spoke as if unaware that I was touching her.

I said through gritted teeth: "I won't risk my poorest legionary for your winter holiday." Angrily I caressed her neck, her shoulders, her thighs. "Fausta, Faustina." She went on staring into the room's dimness, talking, precisely as if I was sitting somewhere over there: talking about whatever came into her head. Her voice had a dry quality. I could tell that her words did not interest her. They were merely sounds thrown up between us. Her stillness and the pallor of her skin increased the illusion of a statue. But under my hands her flesh was warm. If I crushed her breast, I wondered, would she then look at me? My face brushed her hair. I smelt a weak, familiar fragrance. "That scent."

"What scent?"

"Sweet calamus." Depressed, I pushed her away from me and said: "Go and put some on."

Se glanced at me, amused. "I have some on."

"Then put more on. Stink of it."

She climbed down into the room and said: "Haven't you noticed the kind of woman who smells highly of scent?"

I lay back on the bed. "Be that kind of woman." I closed my eyes. My breath was coming in deep sighs. They sounded exasperated above me, like somebody else's. And now, as if to escape the futility of these moments, I remembered a time at

63

Treves reclining at a meal with Fausta and a few others. 'Gaius has a nose like a wolf', she had said. 'He can scent a Persian at two miles, a German at five, and me at ten.' I remembered her laughter and the way she looked at me, almost with love. It now pained me.

This night I dare say I wanted to believe again what I know to be untrue, in herself and in me. Or else it was a reaction from battle. I've heard soldiers say that a day of hatred brings a night of love. Whatever the reason, I felt softened as I heard her approach and smelt the elusive scent – subtle, at least, with my memory. She stood in front of me. She looked rather ashamed, and was rubbing one foot against the other in embarrassment. Her arms covered her breasts. I felt a surge of gentleness for her, almost of adoration. I took her arms lightly in mine. She looked at me, perhaps expecting to see anger or frustration. I don't know what she saw. I kissed her lips, softly. ''Sweet calamus.'' Then I gently kissed her eyes, her lips, her eyes again. ''That's how I fell in love with you.''

She lowered her head, but I had seen the expression on her face. Occasionally, rarely, this happens. Something gives way in her. Then I glimpse a tenderness more moving than that in a naturally tender woman – something frightened and luminous, as if sunlight were breaking over her. These are the words of love, I know. But it is difficult to see clearly, or to write as I do not feel.

She detached herself from me and lay on the bed. It is said that all beauty in our world is the shadow of a heavenly glory, and that our desire for it is the desire for the eternal and the divine. I lay beside this beauty now, and embraced it. I covered its face with kisses. I felt its glow in my hands. I wish these words could hold in them what I knew and felt. But they can't, and it's gone.

She began to laugh. It was her nervous laughter. Laughter at nothing. She tried to sit up, without looking at me. Then she said: ''When are we leaving here? Verona, I mean.'' She shook her hair out of her eyes, yawned, and glanced at the water-clock above the bed. ''In a month we could be in Rome. Then you'll have cleaned the world of its last tyrants.'' She added almost inconsequentially: ''But I'm not saying that about my father. I never said that.''

I stared at her. I suddenly thought: she's guilty at sleeping with her father's enemy, with the man who caused his death.

64

I felt a despair untouched by pity. "Don't mention your father again," I said. "Ever."

She sat upright. "Gaius, I think you're tired."

"I'm not tired, I'm angry." As I watched her sitting above me – she so unreachably herself – I wanted to strike her. I've never hated her so much.

And now this inexplicable woman kissed my lips and said: "Forgive me. I didn't mean to hurt you."

I said fiercely: "I don't know what you're meaning to do."

She smiled down at me with her old warmth. "Don't fight battles with me, Gaius. I surrender."

"Battles!" I cried. "Sarmatian armour's nothing to yours!"

She was shaken by a soft gust of laughter. "Don't hate me. Laugh with me."

I looked away from her, but she took my hands and held their palms to her breasts, wriggling against them. I turned to see her eyes closed in some dream of her own. Even while I was giving her this obscure pleasure she was separate from me. She was writhing alone like a cat, rubbing herself with me as a cat rubs against a door-post. When she noticed me looking at her she made a self-mocking remark. She was in command both of me and of herself. A teasing glitter was in her face. She had turned me into an object.

Furious with resentment, I forced her beneath me on to her back. My touch in her felt dry. But she worked at it dutifully, with her head turned away and her eyes closed. She never makes a sound. While I, angry as so often, betrayed my need in gasps and cries.

XX

Memoranda of Cecrops, servant to Constantine.

[These parchment scraps, in an uneducated hand, devote themselves chiefly to the health and wardrobe of the Augustus.]

9 September

MAJESTY poorly. Evening headaches and hotness in the chest. Apply asphodel with pulp of vinegar and mustard stems. Found dent on shoulder of his breastplate after battle. Told my shock to him. Tell him impossible armourer to repair here. Wait until Rome, says he.

Today Majesty asks me about strength of spells, demons. He complains how everybody contradicts themselves concerning spells. I think to get him wolf's head. Wolf's head is sovereign against all demons, the higher and the lower, say I.

Empress was rude to me. She ordered me out when I was with him, the vixen. I tell Majesty he gets not enough sleep, now he goes to Empress in evening. But Majesty furious.

XXI

The Empress Fausta to her cousin Marina
at Nice.

9 September

MARI, I'm so angry with myself. For the past two days of battle and the city's surrender, I've waited for and thought of Gaius hour after hour. Yes, while he is dictating the future of half the world, I find him worthy of my nature! And then, when he comes at night, I'm cold, almost contemptuous. Why?

I seem not to experience things like other people. They feel in ways I don't understand. Gaius too. He says I'm the only person who's not afraid of him. He doesn't know how he can make me tremble. He sees only the curtain which I lift between us.

Sometimes, when his passion is very searching and gentle, I can't bear it. Then he seems to be spearing me in some part where I am weak. I want to say, like a child: "Not fair!" It does seem unfair. Because then a tenderness spreads inside me – a tenderness (am I explaining it at all?) not to him but to myself. A feeling of *embarrassment*. Isn't that absurd? It seems to be fingering some person who used to be me. Tell me, was I ever a warm child, or soft? Or was I always what you used to call me: Little Boy-Girl?

I suppose it is this other in me who fills me today with longing and frustration. It's happened before. I remember last winter, after Gaius had been angry and passionate with me, walking in the portico of the palace at Treves. He took a handful of snow and

66

pressed it against my face. "That's your love," he said. It burnt
me like fire, as only ice can burn, and filled my head with
confusion. I said yes.

Strange he understood.

XXII

Journal-Memoir of Constantine.

9 September

TOWARDS mid-afternoon my physician came to headquarters
and said that Gallus Verinus was dying. The spear had grazed
the hip-bone and entered his abdomen. The head of it was still
lodged in his side, and had pierced the liver. For a while I could
not steady myself. I've known plenty of grumbling men whose
death would merely complete a process half done. But the death
of Gallus, whose robustness seems to be life itself, was un-
believable. All the weight of the ceiling seemed to be crushing
me inwards. I did not trust myself to speak, but waved the
physician away. When I got up my legs felt numbed.

I reached the field hospital alone. Its tents had been sup-
plemented by others, the wounded were so many, and doctors
called out from Verona. The quiet was unnatural. Gallic
legionaries are noisy and ferocious until they undergo a hospital.
But the moment they find themselves among strange salves and
instruments, they lie very still, their eyes rolling with fear,
hoping the doctors will not notice them. Space was so choked
that the men lay touching one another. There was scarcely room
to walk, and every tent was filled. Many had died on the wagons
which had brought them from the battlefield. When they saw me
there was such a commotion that I imperilled their lives. Many
floundered to their feet with their wounds bleeding again, trying
to touch my hands or my cloak – some in the belief that this
might cure them, others out of loyalty or affection. Those who
could not move, the grey-faced and the dying, saluted me where
they lay.

I found the doctor of the Minervia sterilising instruments over
a flame. He jumped when he saw me and asked to be forgiven for
the hospital's state, as if he were responsible for such carnage.

Verinus was alone in one corner, walled off by bandage-boxes. He lay on a bed covered with blankets and his prefect's cloak. The moment I saw him my breath choked. Already he had the sunken cheeks and eyes I've come to recognise, and his skin was that bloodless twilight colour which sees the end. For a moment he did not notice me, but remained gazing upwards at nothing. Then he turned a face in which the eyes were huge and unlit. His mouth traced a smile.

I sat on the bed and took his hand. Its grip was feeble, cold. He said: "Thank you for sending your physician."

"I sent him without worrying. I thought your wound was light. Why did you tell me it was light?"

"I did not know." His voice was unrecognisable, dwindled to that of an old man. "I was not sure."

"But you had a spear-head in you."

"I've had that before." His smile returned. "Do you remember? Our first year against the Tubanti. In the left shoulder."

For the moment he seemed in no pain, but sometimes his eyes dilated as if they were focusing anew or were surprised. The light I remembered in them – boyish, excitable – was shrunk to an intermittent gleam in their core, almost gone. "I should have recalled what you told me then." That disembodied voice! "Do you remember? You said: watch the enemy on your right; these men sometimes strike outwards. That's what happened last night . . . was it? . . ."

"The night before."

"I was trying to get the standard to hold firm. They were pressing us. A man moved up on my right, to attack the legionary beside me. In the dark I thought he held a sword. But he struck outwards, from five feet away. It was very quick, uncanny. He might have had nothing to do with it."

I tried to recognise in this voice the inflexions I remembered. I could not. And now he talked about our German campaigns, on and on, as if to fix them in his mind like a comfort or a talisman. His eyes remained set on me in their lustreless vacancy. The whiteness of his face was terrible. As he talked I felt as if a part of myself was becoming lost with him. He described, with an oddly exact memory, things which I'd forgotten, but now remembered. When he spoke of the Cherusci he did not mention how he'd saved my life, but I was hit by a pang of helplessness, of guilt, that nothing I could do would save his. By this death, I know now, I am myself in danger of becoming a worse man. It threatens me, because the light of naturalness and sanity, which was his, is one I see fading on all sides. Perhaps my own nature drives it from those around me. Or perhaps it is the old age of the world. I do not know.

For the last few minutes, while he had been talking, he had bent forward from the waist, gasping and closing his eyes. He said suddenly: "You will send my ashes back to Liguria."

It was the first indication that he knew he was dying. He lay back with his head on the pillow again, too exhausted to speak. I shouted for the doctor. Was there nothing to be done, I demanded, no operation which would leave a grain of hope? An unfamiliar pleading sounded in my voice. The doctor is the cleverest of our surgeons: a delicate Syrian, qualified at Alexandria. But he lowered his head. "We drew back the spear-head at once, Eternity; but the liver is already split. The iron is so far in that even if we used the Scoop of Diocles, he would die at once."

He lifted the blankets. Underneath, disfigured by blood and ointments, the flesh of the belly erupted around a splintered shaft, almost hidden. So deep was it embedded that the stomach must have contained almost a foot of iron.

We stared hopelessly. Somebody was screaming at the far end of the tent. Somewhere else voices rose in a chant, singing all together, something solemn and happy. I asked: "Who are those?"

The surgeon said: "Christians."

"What do they sing for?"

"They sing about their god, Augustus. But they die like the rest of us."

He replaced the blankets. The day was darkening and I told him to bring a lamp. Gallus had opened his eyes. They stared above him, and seemed sightless. His lips were moving but for a long time nothing sounded. Then he said: "It's terrible."

"Are you in much pain?"

"No, Gaius. Not that." The voice was more shadowy than ever. "I mean . . . how little I've thought about dying. You'd expect a soldier to think about death . . . but I've never known one who did." Painfully he turned his face to me. "I've gone for

69

years without thinking. . . . I've never really thought. . . . But I tell you what it's like now. Everything seems very little . . . as if it's condensing and moving far away. As if it was never really there at all. It feels as though hardly anything exists. But you exist." He looked at me with heartrending emptiness. "You are sitting there, aren't you?"

"Yes, I'm sitting here." I clasped his hand again. It did not move.

"Gaius, do you believe in women?"

"How do you mean?" I thought he was rambling.

"I mean that they're different from us? Not better, but closer to . . . closer? You remember . . . the women of the Viminal. That's all I regret. I wanted to be married." Some boyish naïveté had reappeared in his face. I was absurdly glad. "I've been looking for this woman, my wife. Odd how clearly I saw her. . . . Is it a lot to miss that, Gaius?"

"No, Gallus, not a lot."

"My brother's wife . . . stank like a leek . . . went to bed with anybody . . . and he thought her wonderful. Perhaps it's worse . . . to be happy and made a fool of." He tried to laugh, but there came only a whispering stutter.

It was almost dark; the surgeon brought a lamp and set it on a bracket near Gallus' head. Its light warmed everything but the glacial face and the hand which lay nervelessly in mine. The screaming in the tent had died to whimpers, like a woman's. The Christians had stopped singing.

Gallus tried to lean towards me. I bent my ear to him. He said weakly: "Is it true that in the Orphic mysteries men have returned from the grave?"

I said: "I never heard that."

"But have they ever returned? I've heard it said a fellow's soul becomes a bee . . . or a nightingale."

I said: "Yes, it's possible." I longed to encourage him but have never felt so helpless. Since childhood the afterlife to me has been an unimaginable shadow, a place to which only others go. I've scarcely thought of it. To my dying soldiers I've said whatever pieties I knew.

Gallus said: "You're close to the Sun, Gaius." The dark blanks of his eyes were feeding on me. "What does He promise?"

He was asking me questions I'd never asked myself. I managed to say: "The Sun is the Lord of life, Gallus. He promises that life will . . . in some way . . . continue." My voice rang hollow to me. I knew I'd failed him. Yes, I – this man whom other men half worship as a god – was unknowing and almost speechless. Because the Sun promises nothing to a dying man. The Sun is for the living. And now it was I, watching the light fade in him, who found myself asking: Where? Where? Can it be, as some believe, that the soul perishes? Or does his life unite with other lives or flower into different forms? Gallus was staring at me now with a stark anguish.

I tried to smile at him but my lips would not stretch. Then suddenly it was he who was smiling at me, wryly, almost naturally. He said: "This will be the first time I've known something before you did. You always knew everything first."

Those were the last words he spoke. A moment later he gave a small sigh, not of pain but of relief, and fell into sleep. For a while I waited in case he should wake up. But his breathing, apart from an unnatural lightness, sounded settled and calm. Piled near his head, his armour was still spattered with the battle's mud, while his sheathed sword, propped against his breast-plate, was hung with an amulet – the charm which had failed him. I picked this up, unfolded the tiny parchment and held it close to the lamp's light. It invoked protection against all demons and sudden dangers, by day or night: 'let them flee the face of the Great God, the mighty Companion, the Sun Invincible'.

At the sixth hour I returned to the hospital. He had not moved but his breathing was lighter, thinner. The doctor said he would not last the night.

Gallus: what is my prayer for you? Not for peace, which would belittle your vitality. No, I pray that you survive death as you are, with the courage and the mind's temper as I remember them. It seems as if in you the last sane voice is stilled. I want you here, but cannot call you back. Comrade, farewell.

XXIII

Commonplace Book of Synesius.

IT's happy to walk in a beautiful city again. The streets are
filled with autumn light. I look at shops, and linger in the baths.
These mercenary Veronese, in all their petty self-seeking, wash
away the memory of blood with a kind of bourgeois innocence.
They sit plump in their doorways surrounded by the impedimenta
of life – children, cats, relatives – as if the siege was quite forgotten. I'm told that many merchants made huge profits bargain-
ing in millet on the black market. And now they cheat our gawky
legionaries, selling them trinkets and false stones.

The amphitheatre is smaller than the Flavian in Rome, but
faced with beautiful marble. At present it is filled with a most
curious noise: the mutter and clinking manacles of thirteen
thousand interned soldiers. In every city we have scooped up
these lethargic garrisons and left behind a quota of men as
gaolers. They will soon exceed our own numbers.

My nostalgia for civilised company took me to the home of my
fellow-Epicurean, the orator Julius. In no time our friendship
had reached its old footing, and we vilified and insulted the world
and one another for a long and happy evening. How miserly
about health old men become! I was delighted to find him more
crippled and immobile than me. He was thrilled to see my hair
gone, while his head is still covered by a white fur (I would not
call it more than that).

He has at last outlived his wife – a great triumph – and his
academic life is over. He tells me that for a long time he has
wanted nothing but to follow out the words of Epicurus: 'Live
unknown.' I observe that with his talents there was little chance
of his living otherwise. He tells me that with mine I was wise to
take service with a half-barbarian emperor. Rudeness in old men
is considered a sign of vitality. In fact it is quite the opposite. It
springs from shrunken sympathies. Julius and I aired these
withered appendages until midnight, and I left feeling better than
in years. But I will not go again.

I walked back through empty streets, wondering if the
Augustus would still be up, and perhaps waiting for me. It is

strange to hear other people talk of him, even Julius. They speak of an edifice, flawless and inhuman. Somehow Constantine projects this. It is as well. Few people can observe him as closely as I do, and every mention of him now makes me deeply uneasy. All the time that he has moved through this country on a tide of success, his mind has been darkening. This darkness runs in a deep opposing current, growing stronger and more dangerous all the time. It cannot be concealed for long.

For a while I thought the arrival of the Empress might alleviate him. Sometimes he behaves as if he loves her, and looks at her with yearning. I wonder what he sees. Every face which we have known long is haunted by its other, younger faces remembered in other times. Does Constantine, perhaps, see in Fausta a gentler woman than she is? Often, even now, she makes him unhappy.

Last night, deepening his pain, the prefect Verinus died of wounds. He was the only legionary prefect one could converse with: not an intelligent man, but amiable and lively.

This evening, as I approached our makeshift offices, I saw a dim light in the Augustus' chambers. He had not yet gone to the Empress, if he would. When I entered he looked at me with such a sad, heavy expression that I guessed he had been brooding on Verinus.

I said: "You must sleep, Eternity."

But he ignored this and demanded at once: "Tell me, Synesius, did you ever hear that in the Orphic mysteries men returned from the dead?"

"No, my lord, never." I don't know where he could have learnt this. I once knew a disbarred initiate of the mysteries, who told me that all he had to do was to eat a sacrificial meal of bull's flesh, which gave him a bad stomach-ache.

The Augustus looked disconsolate. Small, tired pockets depressed the corners of his mouth. "Then what do these cults know of the world beyond," he asked, "the mysteries of Osiris, Cybele and the rest?"

I hesitated. "They teach the brotherhood of life, Augustus, that men after death are reunited with the Infinite, and with the process of eternal re-creation."

Constantine was glowering at me. He hates sophistry, but I didn't know what else to say. "You mean a man dies, then? The individual dies? The intellect. The heart. The body. They die?" Under his close beard the powerful chin was grinding back and forth. "Do I understand you right?"

"Not precisely die, my lord, no." My voice sounded odd to me, it tiptoed. "The single life is absorbed in the universal life."

"Universal!" He half stood up. He was shaking with anger and disappointment, not at me but at this phantasmal hereafter. "Absorbed! Then this Oneness is just a pseudonym for extinction!" He glared at me. "We become Nothing. Or Everything. Can it matter which, if neither is anything? It's all nonsense, then, just nonsense of the mind?"

I said: "Yes, Augustus. I think that those who desire it are out of love with life. They desire not only to escape this existence, but any at all."

He sat down heavily. "These cults, then, offer no more than the Sun." This remark, I think, cost him effort. For these last days, I suspect, he has been so bewildered by this god of his that he refuses to contemplate him. And it is true that the cult of the sun offers just such a cycle: the impersonal regeneration of crops and mankind. It amazes me still how people marvel at and sanctify such obvious things. They emerge from crypts and temples holding sheaves of sacred corn or dripping with bulls' blood and cry *Eureka!* to what the poorest common sense would have told them.

I was cruelly conscious of not comforting the Augustus. The gritted tightness in his face was only more pronounced, and his eyes smarting.

"Death is harmless," I ventured. "As long as we exist, it is not there. And when it comes, we are not there. It is impossible to experience."

The Augustus said curtly: "That answers nothing."

I felt I could not help him any more. Certainly I could not give him what he wanted to hear. People tell me I am cynical, but in a weak-minded age that is often said of men who recognise facts. The weakness of the Augustus is that he cannot believe in the insignificance of things. He talks of Fate and of what is meant to be. It does not occur to him that there may be no Fate, and that nothing is meant. Why should the Powers, if there are any, hold council on human affairs? That is an invention of man's twin illnesses: his vanity and his terror of the dark.

74

The grief-stricken face of the Augustus moved but could not alter me. Such endless toying with deities and destinies must sap him in the end. Only a person of his energy could have supported it so long, and won half a war as well.

"You must think of the men now, my lord, and the campaign," I said, and to my own surprise found myself quoting at him:

"'We have an instant now to please the living,
    But all eternity to love the dead.'"

But the Augustus, of course, has never read Sophocles, and I do not think he even heard me.

XXIV

The Lady Politta to the Lady Lucia Balba
at Turin.

11 September

I EXPECT you've heard by now, Biji, that we've been in a *battle*. It was only ten miles away and honestly, in Verona you could hear a mouse squeak. We all thought we were going to die except, of course, for the Empress, who I suppose can't imagine anything so undignified occurring to her. She sat on the villa rooftop with that dreadful old Synesius, both of them as cool as cats, discussing how to burn the state papers.

But now all the poor brave boys are back — or most of them. Yesterday from my carriage I noticed them washing at cauldrons. You've never seen such bodies, Biji — so *muscular*, and scarred like paving-stones. And of course we've been introduced to the generals. How I wish you could have been there! There's a wart-faced praetorian prefect and a bandy-legged cavalry commander and a little shrimp of a Master of the Offices and oh, lots more. The Empress says that Wart-Face is one of the finest soldiers in the Empire, and that the Shrimp is *deadly*. I do think it's *extraordinary* that all these men can look as they do and still be so important, don't you? My poor dear Cornelius always used to say you could see a man's honour in his face. But not any more.

Today we're packing up ready to move on Aquileia and then

south. Everything's so frustrating. The Empress is very moody. Most of the morning she sat about in a dream, which isn't like her at all. It seems unfair, just when we're all moving and the servants need orders, but it's no good my saying anything. Of course I'm a little her senior [this is understatement; the Lady Politta was thirty-seven, the Empress twenty-four] but she listens to nothing I say. I think something's happened between her and the Augustus. Aren't men *beastly*? I'm sure the Empress is right to hate them. (At least I think she hates them.) I never look at the Augustus without shaking. He's like a crag moving about.

But I don't know what the trouble can be with them. She's always vivid with him and they talk a lot together. In fact they both seem very correct. Such a change after the Milan set, where everybody walked about so importantly all day, but you knew that at night they took off their clothes and went to bed with the most *extraordinary* people, and did peculiar things.

XXV

Hosius, Bishop of Cordoba, to Victor of Ulia,
Priest.

11 September

GREETINGS, dearest brother. By God's grace Verona has surrendered, and we have won a great battle on the plain to the east.

But the number of the wounded is terrible. They lie in tents with no priest of theirs to comfort them, and many die like this, in fear. I have spent all day with the Christians amongst them, reading to some and confessing others. But the confessions of these men are perplexing. They will forget how many women they have raped or how many men they have killed, yet the theft of a sandal from some fellow-soldier haunts their souls. One of the tribunes, badly wounded and in great pain, confided to me that he too had once been of our number, but had joined the brotherhood of Mithras during the great persecution. I know that he wished to return to us, but his time was too short. They gave him a skinful of wine and a coin to bite on, and amputated his leg above the knee. He never regained consciousness.

Today I was summoned to audience with the Augustus. This was very strange. We walked for a way beyond the camp, quite alone, he dressed only in the simplest tunic like a leader of the old Republic. He spoke more quietly than usual and his face looked dulled. He told me that he was grieved by the death of a comrade-in-arms. I felt very moved. I had not realised the Emperor was such a lonely man. And since he walked in a long silence, I ventured to say what we all know: that no man has greater love than he who sacrifices his life for his friends.

But the Augustus was furious. "Friends? Friends?" he shouted. "He was a professional soldier! He gave his life for nobody." But what he was really saying, I think, was: how dare you speak to me without being addressed first!

So for a long time more we walked among the trees near the river. The Augustus kept looking up at them with an odd misery. It is impossible to tell what is passing in his mind. Eventually he asked me why we Christians ignored the sun. His anger had gone and he seemed interested in my reply. I had a feeling that he was uncertain of everything. I told him truly that all our churches were orientated to the sunrise, that our day of prayer was the Sunday and that the sun is the prince of God's creations.

He seemed neither pleased nor displeased. He stopped with his hands against a tree trunk and fondled its bark. I had never seen him like this. Then he said: "Where is this man Verinus now? What do your books say?"

This was hard, my brother. The dead man was a sun-worshipper like the Augustus himself. It is inconceivable that he entered paradise. Yet who was I to say he burnt in Hell? The Augustus has a way of looking which is very hard on a man. He uses his stare like a weapon. But I managed to say: "It is not mine to know, Eternity. I know only that his spirit is imperishable."

"It does not dissolve into nature?"

"No, Augustus. It remains itself."

"How? Is it like the shades of the Elysian Fields, a half-man? Or is it like certain priests say, a kind of incorporeal . . . nothing?"

It occurred to me then, my brother, how beautiful is our

doctrine of the resurrection of the body. The body is the partner of the soul and together they must burn or be transfigured. How much more complete will be our joy in paradise! We will see again the faces of those we loved, hear their voices and feel their hands. Yes, we shall embrace them, body and spirit.

So I told the Emperor fervently: "No, Augustus, our afterlife is not a world of ghosts. We are alone among religions in this: we believe that the soul puts on a celestial body. Yes, everything is preserved. All the qualities of spirit, mind and flesh, except for sin. Nothing is lost, my lord!"

The Augustus, dear friend, is a man of literal mind and small imagination, and I could tell that this holy doctrine appealed to him deeply. He stared and smiled at me very kindly, with an expression of wondering and suppressed hope. But he said: "Isn't the body a burden? Isn't it better shed?" And he added in a slightly threatening voice: "How, in any case, can it be re-assembled, after being scattered to ashes or eaten by vultures?"

I think the force of his words only reached him after he had said them, because suddenly his face clouded and his hands clenched together.

I said: "The earthly body is shed, Eternity. The soul is clothed in its heavenly counterpart. We must not attribute to God the inabilities of men."

This was bold to say. But the Augustus did not answer, only started to walk back through the trees. His mood was elusive. I sensed a hesitant warmth towards me. At last he put his hand on my shoulder in a most natural way and said: "How do you know these things?"

I said: "They come from history, Augustus. Our God Himself was resurrected. That is how we know."

I saw him frowning. His hand fell to his side. "This Jesus, you mean? A Galilean peasant executed for treason?"

There are times when it is wiser not to answer. The Augustus, I have noticed, is not interested in theory or dogma. He is a very practical man. Only where divinity touches his personal interest – his grief or his need for support – does he listen to its voice. At all other times his mind is lax and confused.

He would make God his slave.

As we emerged from the trees I saw that the Minervia legion was assembling in the open space west of our earthworks. They were preparing for the cremation of their prefect. The Augustus walked slowly towards them staring at the ground, myself following. I think he had forgotten I was with him. He did not speak again.

XXVI

Journal-Memoir of Constantine.

11 September

SCARCELY ever do I feel what I am expected to feel. Twice I have wept at weddings, and once laughed out loud at the funeral of a relative. At my greatest military victory I was sick; at my marriage I felt nothing. And today, when six thousand men march behind the bier of Gallus Verinus, and I am the symbol of the army's honour and gratitude, I experience no rush of praise or pride for him. Instead I miss a friend: a tone of voice, a way of laughing.

We marched in a light dust. The melancholy of the horns and trumpets preceded us in the distance. I followed the bier, with the legionary tribunes, who clasped my hand and spoke the ancient phrase: "He is happy." All day I accept platitudes as truth. But today this "He is happy" filled me with wonder at the poverty of our hearts. Who had really thought what he was?

When we reached the pyre I mounted a dais and Tetricus thrust into my hands the speech which some secretary had written as a panegyric. I looked across the glittering lake of men. The speech was long, and it had to be bellowed. There is a peculiar madness about shouted hypocrisy. Its mere volume convinces. I cut off my mind from it. The words floated beyond me in a voice not my own. They belonged to imperial rhetoric and spoke of glory. Once or twice I could hear Verinus laughing at some sentence, as if he and I were alone. I glanced only once at the bier; its pale fragment of man seemed to have nothing to do with him. I fixed my stare on the horizon. The speech's words galloped obscenely about. ". . . Followed his Emperor . . . like Ajax of old . . . a matchless and incalculable valour . . . died for his Emperor. . . ."

79

A sticky heat was rising between my breastplate and my chest. I wanted to scratch. The absence of the man I knew, absent more than ever in these words, began to turn to agony under that senseless sky. The men's armour glimmered feebly below and far away. I stared up. The Sun was too bright to look at. He bathed the world in indifference. 'The Sun doesn't speak.' Nothing spoke. Only the madness of eulogy. And all the time around its dishonesty, like a haunting vapour, breathed the unanswered Where? Where? My chest was constricted and burning. I felt its sweat sliding down my ribs. For 'a loyal and mighty devotee of the Empire' I substituted "a cheerful comrade". And now there came a description of our campaign against the Cherusci, like a battle from *The Iliad*. Just as I was shouting about the shining invincibility of his countenance, there pounced on me a memory so vivid I could hardly continue. I saw a ring of savage faces in the forest darkness, and heard my own gasping breath. And breaking through, the face of Gallus pouring sweat and dirt. 'Come on, Gaius, hack through. Hack through or we're done.'

I stepped off the dais as if into emptiness. The bier was placed on the pyre. His upturned face held no expression, unless of faint repudiation. I opened and closed his eyes, and kissed him farewell. His cloak and armour were already piled at his feet. I summoned the torchbearer and lit the wood.

Fire is a mystery. None of our philosophers or scientists, I think, has come close to explaining it. It belongs to the divine. I reflect that the Sun Himself is fire, and burns, perhaps, with the invincible constancy of God. But even this I no longer know. And if it is true, it happens with the same indifference to men as the furnace now consumed Verinus. While the tribunes threw incense into the flames, I prayed for his soul. But my prayer was undirected, like an arrow shot into the night. Where God is, what He wills and how He acts has become clouded to me. I am given a thousand answers, but no certainties. Our whole age sinks in confusion.

Cremation is like a second death. The muscles tauten in the heat so that the corpse raises its arms among the flames and tries to sit up. Disintegration is total. The skull cracks, the brains spill out, the limbs drop off. Within an hour the body is ashes and blown air. The tribunes watched in a spellbound gloom. Some of the legionaries – Germans – sent up an unearthly, high-pitched whine, and clashed their spears.

I kept my gaze beyond the fire, staring at the lank pines and the yellowing grass. These too, I thought, will decay and become Gallus. The dead are everything, nothing. I thought of my conversation with Synesius. His beliefs are cold, and I find myself not hearing what he says. I seem not to listen to words, but to personality. Perhaps that is why the bishop warms me. Compared to him Synesius is unpardonably old.

My eyes strayed to the charred shadow of Gallus. I thought of the celestial body. A group of hooded crows settled among the pines in evil omen. So I went on imagining the heavenly counter-part, shaped in light, sinless. That vision filled me with a momentary comfort. I wanted to believe it. I did, a little. I indulged it. I thought of my father, frail on his deathbed in York, but now restored by some beneficence of heaven.

But I cannot create a truth because I need it. Synesius quotes Epicurus and says that the memory of a good friend is sweet. Yet even this banality is false. The memory is grief. After an hour we quenched the flames in wine and I sent the urn with the ashes of Verinus back to his family in Liguria.

Ever since then, in pain, I have tried to think of the celestial body.

For the last time I sit at this table before Verona while the night grows late. Tomorrow we march south. It is strange that on its surface everything seems good. The army is confident and strong. I received the surrender of Aquileia this morning without loss of men or time. The road opens on Rome through plentiful country in clement weather.

Our troubles are all unseen. My face is a mask of sweat in the cool night. My fingers shake. My doctor says I'm healthy as a bull. Sometimes my eyes physically see a darker landscape than I know exists. When I close them they ache behind their lids, as if they were bruised. I wish I could tell if this was natural or inflicted from outside. Priests say that demons first affect the eyesight. But I don't know whether I am more vulnerable if I contemplate or ignore Maxentius. Is awareness a safeguard? Or do my own thoughts imperil me?

Sometimes, as though from a great height, I imagine my legions trickling like ants on the road to Rome. They do not realise that no divinity supports them. They go into a threatening void, and their vulnerability terrifies me. But I no longer know how to act. I simply continue as I first intended, and seem now to have no choice but to march against the elder gods of Rome beneath a Sun which has turned cold.

PART TWO

✳

TO ROME

I

The Empress Fausta to her cousin Marina.

Hostiglia, 14 September

WE move through a ghostly country. The peasants have all
fled and the land is covered in mist so that we cannot see
more than half a mile ahead. This is the Po valley, which is
famous for wheat and whose houses are the weirdest you ever
saw, standing on piles. Livilla and I have opened both windows
of our carriage, and stare out into whiteness. I confess it's a little
frightening. The flooded river moves in sickles of light over the
plain. We see it dimly as we advance into the haze – slabs of grey
sheen, and lagoons where half-drowned trees stand.

Two or three times a day Gaius rides by with his staff. The
rest of the time we rely for news on the commander of my
guard, a bloodless little man, very courteous. This news is all
good. Aquileia has surrendered, Hostiglia has surrendered. Gaius
says everyone surrenders to him except me. I ignore this jibe.

We're travelling very light. The whole court retinue is much
reduced. I left most of my servants and wardrobe behind at
Verona, and was glad to shed my eunuchs, who were gossiping
like turkeys. It's interesting how little baggage one needs. In any
case I have recently been affecting a stark simplicity of dress,
since Livilla covers herself in jewels. She was very upset at our
leaving so much behind. But she has now dyed her hair with a
most flamboyant *spumo*, and is recovered. When she gazes out of
the window she is not looking at scenery. No, I'm afraid she has
a yearning for the Summoenium [prostitution] and flirts continually with my coarser officers. I think she literally pestered
her poor, dear Cornelius to death.

So we continue south. Our carriage idles, to keep pace with

the men. We go in the centre of the army among the court baggage, while behind us roll the siege engines: wall-borers and wild-asses and battering-rams all drawn by oxen. You've never seen such an array. The rattle of their wooden wheels is terrible over the paving-slabs and the oxen moan and bellow with the misery of it. But in front of us the cohorts move in an eerie silence. Their armour glimmers oddly in the haze. They are like a march of ghosts, but tall and savage ones, strong as trees.

Gaius and I spent last night together. He was overcome by a grim abstraction. He feels we're marching into an intangible wall. The clouding of the Sun disquiets him even more than its presence. I don't know how to help him, or what to say. He is brooding, too, over the death of Verinus, our best prefect, and asked me about the Christian doctrine of the resurrected body. But you know how ignorant I am about these things. What was it, Marina, do you know?

How I hate myself when I am with him sometimes! I find my patience sapping. The way he flails about among abstractions! One moment he fills me with awe, the next I am exasperated. But half the time I don't know whether he is being stupid or I. I see things so simply. And when I watch him with the army I realise that compared to him I'm an infant.

Sometimes, Mari, I feel a traitor with Gaius, almost as if I am spying. Because to a part of him I'm a stranger, and always will be. And I think the difference is this: Gaius is fundamentally good, while I, like Maxi, am not. You see, *my brother and I are alike*. Neither of us has ever craved for the light. When Gaius falls into a turmoil about his God, I hear my brother's mocking laughter. I admire Gaius, but I understand Maxi. Oh Mari – I even start to laugh myself, inwardly. Isn't that terrible? Yes, I join in that mockery! I can see Maxi's dog-head thrown back on his shoulders. Laughing and laughing!

Mari, I must stop this.

Here's something happier, which I mustn't forget to tell you. We had dinner yesterday with the sacred retinue in the posting-house where we were camped – and Hosius and Synesius discovered one another! I promise you, this was better than gladiators! In fact it was quite unprecedented. They were reclining uneasily opposite one another. Even in looks they are ridiculously opposite. Hosius is flaccid and round like a eunuch, and overflows wherever he is; whereas Synesius looks so dried and small you feel he's been artificially preserved for the winter.

It began with Hosius boasting about the number of Christians in the army. "Is this so?" remarks Synesius caustically. "Who then was it said 'You shall not kill'?" He had probably tolerated Hosius talking for a long time, because somewhere deep in him, like a worm in dead wood, I think there was anger. He went on to remark that the insane idealism of Christianity obliged Christians to be hypocritical and that no wonder the religion appealed to house-slaves.

The bishop replied in his too-smooth voice: "We say that the sword came into the world because of injustice. It is a necessary evil."

Synesius wriggled upright on his couch. His legs dangled down like a child's. "That is typical of the contradictions in your faith," he said.

The bishop was unperturbed. In fact imperturbability is his essence. I don't think I like him. He issued a bland challenge: "What are the contradictions in my faith?"

I saw Synesius' little eyes ignite. This man, I must tell you, is an extraordinary fund of knowledge, some of it fascinating and most of it quite useless. He obviously knew so many contradictions that for a moment he couldn't select one. Then he picked the cruellest he could think of and replied: "Your Nazarene threatened eternal punishment to unbelievers, but he himself said that people will receive in the same measure as they mete out." He paused a second, needling the bishop with his eyes. "From this I would conclude that the Nazarene is himself in hell." He glanced at us to judge if we were displeased, but Gaius was watching with a half-smile, holding a mullet uneaten in his fingers. Synesius, encouraged, then appeared to address himself to the room: "But what can you expect? After all, who was this man? A Jewish ascetic rabbi, not untypical of his day. He cannot be counted as a philosopher, he is too unsophisticated. Socrates would have left him not merely in dialectic pieces, but quite uncomprehending."

I watched the bishop in the hope of seeing discomfort, but he seemed invulnerable to it. He rolled off his couch and stood with one hand at his chest. "This is Christ's strength!" he boomed.

"He spoke to the people, in stories. Yes, he was simple and emotive. I am proud to say so."

"And today it is only simple people who admire him," said Synesius, with measured rudeness. "He does not appeal to the intellect. All your books are filled with contradictions, bishop. I could give you a hundred more!"

The bishop did not invite this. He assembled his robes majestically about his feet and eased his hands over his stomach. He said simply, but with a rather moving conviction: "The books you speak of, Secretary, were written by God."

"If that is so," Synesius answered, "then God writes in a most indifferent Greek. Even his history is faulty."

But now the bishop steered himself towards the centre of the semi-circle of couches. He too was watching us, and bowed courteously. His black eyes were creased about with fat and twinkled out very small at Synesius. He exudes a chubby comfort, but I suspect he is calculating. "You accuse us of contradictions," he said, "but what is more contradictory than your multiplicity of gods? I've heard it said that these gods are like many paths, all of them leading to light. But is that so? Consider the shape of these divinities! Mithras, born of fire and a stone. . . ." And he went on to unravel an endless list of cults and deities, carefully omitting the Sun and Jupiter. I must say, Marina, spoken of like that they sounded alien even to me. I can't remember half of them, but he ended in a flush of rhetoric: "A hundred major gods and a myriad minor ones! The stars, the earth, the harvest! Spirits of trees and rivers! Gods demanding blood, wine, virginity! Compound and synthetic gods, human-headed and monster-bodied, monster-headed and human-bodied, gods who are lords of All and lords of nothing! The deities honoured long ago as the guardians of the Republic have been drowned in the flotsam of the conquered world!"

It was a very bold speech, and it may have earned him enemies. I noticed the Marshal, who follows Mithras, chewing angrily on nothing. But the bishop was watching Gaius, who long ago repudiated all but the Sun. And now he stood in front of our couch, bowed again, and said very quietly to us: "Can these be manifestations of the divine, Augustus? Are they not demons, rather, or at least no more a god than I am?"

Synesius looked ruffled. He had slid off his couch too, and

hung about the flanks of Hosius, like a wasp attacking a toad. Unfortunately there is something comical about him. He wears his beard long and straggling, as if he was in mourning, and his whole head is crooked forward. "And your Jesus," he said, "a criminal executed by Rome for sedition! What is that for a god?" The white hair flared out in wisps round his bald head. "You affect to despise these cults, but Christianity is itself a medley of them. I think merely of your god's resurrection."

I sensed Gaius' quickened interest beside me. I knew he was thinking of Verinus. He was staring intently into his wine-cup in a way I recognised, so that all the bones of his face seemed to be throbbing up under the flesh, tautening it. The other men – mostly court officials – looked either angry or bemused.

Synesius went on: "At the rites of Attis and Cybele in Rome, which I remember well from my childhood, the effigy of a young god was mourned and laid in a sepulchre. Then at night a light shone, the tomb was revealed empty and the god risen. His followers – my mother was one – would hail this as a token of their own immortality." He pointed his finger disdainfully at Hosius. "I wonder if the bishop recognises this tedious myth? And of course the rites of Adonis, Osiris and others are similar. And all this began centuries before your Nazarene, bishop. Centuries! Oh your death and resurrection! A hundred petty Syrian gods have promised as much. They die and are reborn with the turning of the seasons. It's as old as man."

"Those gods," replied the bishop, "died, as you say, for the renewal of the earth. Their worshippers merely partake in the cosmic cycle." He turned to Gaius. "But our God died for men's spirits, for the resurrection of the soul. While those other gods shuffle a dead man into nothing, ours preserves him for ever."

Out of the side of my eye I watched Gaius' fingers stroking his cup. They moved with a delicate intensity. I said, to comfort him: "Perhaps that is right."

Synesius was looking cynically round the room. "I once took pains to read the four Christian accounts of the resurrection of this god," he said, "but they contradicted each other so much that I gave up in amazement."

Gaius stared at the bishop. But Hosius answered at once: "That is because they are living history, not blank philosophy,

Secretary!" He smiled around him, brimming with confidence. "Yes, they are life! Life!"

I did not hear Synesius reply, because Gaius suddenly took my hand and kissed it and said: "No wonder Hosius is such a happy man." He looked pleased, and newly calm. I thought he watched that oily bishop with something like affection. This irritated me. And when I next turned to listen it was to hear Hosius bursting with enthusiasm.

"You say these miracles are impossible," he cried. "But is not the whole of life a miracle? The stars, the falling leaves, the shape of a man's thoughts!" He was ecstatic. "Anaxagoras said that the sun was larger than the Peloponnese. In his day people were shattered and incredulous. Today we are ready to believe him. What is there more extraordinary than the world in which we live, or than we who live in it? The mind of a man can no more compass a cat than a cat can compass a man. All the universe is a miracle!"

Synesius said drily, as if offering him help: "What is it you wish to know about a cat?"

But the bishop rushed on: "Where is reason? Your own Plato claimed that 'the sane man is nowhere at all compared with the madman', and even Socrates had a familiar which surpassed his intellect." *et cetera, et cetera*.

Oh Marina, what a feast it was after the clank and dust of travel and the stink of bloodshed! And isn't it strange how one man can express an idea forcefully, while in the mouth of another the same words would come to grief? They were both, I confess, moving and comical by turns.

And it was now that Synesius must have decided it was useless to argue. For the first time he moved into the centre of our tiny, incidental stage and drew himself upright. It was strange what a silence he made by simply standing there, he is so small. He turned and appealed to Caius and me. The cynicism had quite left his voice. It was touched instead by an odd dignity and sadness.

The Christians, he said, longed only for a world to come – a sapless eternity which had about it all the lassitude and improbability of perfect peace. He did not so much as glance at the bishop. "We were not born for that state," he said, "we could not endure it. We were born for this one. The Christians, by repudiating it, inflict a slight on God's creation, and a blasphemy to the beauty and variety of the world. And their certainty that they are right makes them more than ever wrong. They are merely mourners at the funeral of life. Nowhere can I find in them the openness, wisdom and gentleness of our early philosophers, or the grandeur and innocence of Homer. They are filled only with sin and chastisement, confession and cleansing. They create guilt, then offer their faith as its redemption. It is an ugly cycle. It builds on fear. It belittles man. Yet it is not by chance, I think, that this religion has grown powerful among us. No. It has arisen because the light of our own world has turned thin, and is fading into its night.''

How absurdly dissimilar, dear cousin, is what we say from what we are! Here was Synesius, so withered, so lifeless, lauding the radiance of the world. And there was Hosius, jolly and corpulent as a jellied frog, embracing the faith of ascetics. But I confess I was stirred.

For the first time the look of optimism vanished from the bishop's features and was replaced by insult and passion. His whole face and neck were quivering and blushing. ''Joyless and belittling!'' He lifted his hand. Then he threw himself in front of us, tearing back his robes from his chest, and cried: ''Are these the scars of a lacklustre man? Forgive me, Augustus, but these I suffered for the faith your Secretary scorns! Am I then a madman?'' When he turned his back I saw that it was covered by a maze of livid scars.

Marina, I seem to have been alone in thinking there was something obscene about it. Every eye was riveted on the bishop. And the presence and certitude of this man, I must admit, were impressive, even though his back was covered not only with scars but with strange little curly hairs, like pigs' tails.

Afterwards Gaius told me that he thought Hosius by far the more striking man. While I, for all his quaintness, incline to Synesius. My husband had listened all the time with rapt attention. I noticed the tendons moving about inside his cheeks, just as they do when he's sexually aroused. Later he became abstracted, and once said: ''Only a powerful god keeps a servant like that.'' Like his father he has always had a weakness for this despised religion. And it's exasperating that this fat Spanish Jew, or whatever he is, has all the certainty that Gaius lacks. I think this aggravates Gaius too. Do you remember as a child how disconcerting it was to find a junior doing something better than you? It made her a little uncanny.

Something I nearly forgot to add. Last night, after the rest had gone, I heard a noise in the main room of the posting-house. I looked in and saw Gaius pouring out a libation. When I asked the reason he replied: "I think Synesius blasphemed."

It is late now, and I must end. We are camped beyond Hostiglia, and have already crossed the Po – a swollen calm of a river, 'the mother of Cisalpine Gaul', as they say. The whole valley is lush with it, like one great sluggish womb.

Today my seamstress told me how to stop darkness under the eyes: lapserpicium with a paste of myrrh and lupin seeds. I'll tell you how it does.

II

Journal-Memoir of Constantine.

14 September

TWO-DAY march to Hostiglia through heavy mist. Change to the Vegetian order of march: legionary cavalry in advance; then German auxiliaries; three legions; baggage, court, siege-engines; Augusta legion.

The Po valley navigable, covered with dykes and lagoons; reminds me of Lower Egypt. The tributaries of the Tartarus river dissipate in marsh here. Bridges still standing. Ample grain and salt for supplies. The mist covers our approach, and we go fast. Four hundred miles from Rome.

At noon today heard that our cavalry had surprised enemy engineers trying to demolish the bridge over the Po. Cavalry secured the passage. The bridge, by a miracle, was untouched. We arrived in early evening to find the river very full. Received the surrender of Hostiglia, and small garrison.

The weather oppressive. The sun is glazed or absent. I find myself looking up continuously, but without hope. Last night we camped in an imperial posting-house, where the Bishop of Cordoba defended his god. Very moving. He is the only cheerful spiritual influence around me. For the first time I think of Gallus with hope.

South of the Po. The road runs flat and straight through fields of wheat stubble. The harvests are all in. This is a healthy province: fat, alluvial soil, good for cereals and wine. But even so the canals show signs of silting, and I hear the agricultural slaves are few and old. These symptoms paradoxically ease me. Rome is declining, and needs a master. I have thought this for many years. We march through huge estates owned by senators and palatine officials. I talk to the Master of the Offices and he agrees that the farming is not as intensive as in Gaul. Peasant proprietors are rare now. There's a shortage of labour every-where, and tax concessions to the rich cripple the tenant farmer.

[Here follow observations on fiscal and land reform.]

In this haze it's more than ever necessary to ride the length of the army. So several times a day I see Fausta's carriage: white horses in the mist. Lumbering among so many men, it touches me with pride. Her face in the window looks always calm and intelligent. For a few minutes' conversation I forget the tension between us. She asks questions and gives ideas. While we talk an excitement burns in her. I believe she'd like to be riding with me.

Curious incident on today's march. An old woman limped over the fields towards us and pleaded to the passing legionaries to tell her what had become of her son, Rugda the Suionean. For three hours, dressed in rags, she stood begging by the road as the army went by. The men considered her mad. But later I heard that conquered Germans had been settled on this land by the Emperor Probus thirty years before, and that several of our legionaries had relatives here. Rugda the Suionean had risen to be a centurion of the Primigenia, but had been killed on the Rhine fifteen years ago.

At noon I heard confirmation that our fleet, deploying round Sicily, has failed to stop the Egyptian grain transports reaching Rome. It also came to my notice that officers have reported false quotas of their dead to the quartermaster, and have been appropriating extra rations and allowances. In my disappointment at the fleet's failure I issued some harsh sentences, then retracted them. Feel bitter with the day's frustration.

We press forward to Modena, which has closed its gates against us.

4 days later

It occurs to me that war has something in common with pantomime. Thus, the siege of Modena. We made a show of our assault-weapons and hurled some rocks. The enemy sallied out to pour Greek fire on our ballistas, but instead set himself alight and retired. For another day he watched us from the ramparts, moving from point to point so we might think him more numerous than he is. My own men went through a tedious charade of building earthworks. The gates opened and the city surrendered with honour.

I was approached gingerly by the prefecture, and a nurtured lot they were. Nowhere will you see riches more grossly written than in the face of an Italian sheep-farmer. The prefect himself kissed my feet, then stood up and said through a mouth full of gold teeth: "Our city cannot resist your might, my Eternal Lord." In that one scented face I could diagnose the decline of the whole Empire. Had he resisted he would doubtless have suffered and the city eventually been taken. So his surrender was only sensible. Yet if every petty governor stopped being sensible and held out against me, I'd have no more chance of winning this campaign than of conquering India.

Question: how to infuse love and heroism into one's subjects?

I know no answer to this, but I considered it at length while my panegyric was delivered by an orator from the gateway of Modena. The eulogy is an inescapable part of the pantomime: "Worthy descendant of Dardanus and the noble kings of Troy (this absurdity, culled from my Dardanian origins, was new to me), true son of Apollo, saviour of Gaul, terror of the Bructeri and crusher of the Franks. . . ." I examined the faces of the city councillors opposite me. I've never seen such food for Styx. Their nervousness showed only in the fidgeting of their manicured hands. Their lips were smiling very earnestly. My own staff too were smiling dutifully at this person whom the orator conjured. Through my father I had become a descendant of the Emperor Claudius Gothicus. The bridge I had thrown across the Rhine was more memorable than that of Xerxes over the Hellespont. My name struck terror into the uncouth barbarian breast *et cetera*.

Should I become emperor in Rome, I wondered, how will I remain a proper man? If I banish all flatterers I'll rule an empty city. Just then I remembered Fausta. She had not shown herself, but her carriage stood close, and its window had eased open. As I noticed her, she lifted up her eyes in mock reverence, and grimaced at me.

III

Commonplace Book of Synesius.

21 September

AT the surrender of Modena a most insinuating panegyric claimed as an ancestor for Constantine – who? The Emperor Claudius the Goth-Slayer, no less. This gives him a hereditary right to the Empire far superior to that of Maxentius, and was delivered with such brazen insouciance that it will no doubt start a legend. Already the gossips of the court camp are saying that Constantine's father was a blue-blooded Flavian and his mother a lady of substance. I see history, once the art of fact, being traduced before my eyes into the science of flattery. Because everyone knows that Constantine's father was the son of a goatherd and a freedman's daughter, and that the Lady Helena was a barmaid. And who *her* father was, *nobody* knows. I could not glimpse the face of the Augustus while this was going on, though I imagine his eyes were closed in their well-simulated ecstasy.

It is years since I suffered the Italian ooze and persiflage. Only a day elapses between the city's capitulation and our departure, yet in that time a hundred petitions have arrived in my office from men expecting redress for their pettiest wrongs. We are conquering Italy and they tell us about their cabbages.

No sooner had the city been pardoned than the Augustus and court officials were invited to a banquet at the prefecture. Such resilience! The men whom Constantine might have executed this morning were dining him this evening. But he wants the city's goodwill, so we found ourselves reclining for five irretrievable hours in the most odious company. I was placed once again not far from the unctuous Bishop of Cordoba, while those on my other side were engrossed in talk of real-estate. But the food was superb: peacocks' eggs in sturgeon sauce, and duck done with dates, honey and wine; Armenian apricots. The Augustus and the Empress were raised on a couch a little above the rest. Behind them the Emperor's old servant Cecrops, either through greed or zeal, was most obtrusive in his food-tasting: an idiotic custom in our days of subtle poisons, merely securing the death of two people instead of one.

The Augustus, for once, looked mellow and relaxed. The fingers of one hand pattered absently on the Empress' arm. She, I think, enjoys these occasions. She likes to organise, or to show off. In camp she has little chance, but broods in her tent like Achilles, and writes letters to friends in Gaul which are doubtless intercepted by the secret police of the Augustus. She was looking as usual, pale and animated. They say she had a strange childhood; her parents hated her.

I don't remember how I again became enticed into conversation with that witless bishop. I suppose I had a choice between sheep-farming on one side of me and Jesus on the other. I noticed him smiling at me in a most smug way. I think he thought he was radiating forgiveness. In a while he started to talk about the infallibility of his scriptures. I told him roundly that the story of the Galilean was quite lost and that it was impossible to know who this prophet thought he was, only what his followers wished him to be. Christ, I reminded the bishop, was not a Christian. He was an orthodox Jew, who set himself up as the messiah – a common delusion of the time – and who was misguided enough to think he could evaporate Roman rule in Palestine by a pacifist rebellion. But seeing the bishop still smiled his smug smile, I added I had no quarrel with Christ but that the Christians were insufferable.

Scientists have held that fat reduces sensitivity. This theory appealed to me as I watched the bland pumpkin of the bishop's face mouthing bombast as if I had not spoken. At last his talk of charity became unbearable. His voice reminds me of something slithering over marble. I told him: "Your faith can never be truly loving, bishop, because it implies that all those born before its time have lived and perished without meaning. That is an affront to kindly men."

At this he resorted to some sophistry about baptism in hell, and I told him that baptism had been cribbed by Christianity from the mystery religions along with everything else. I was pleased to see that I'd needled him. The blackcurrant eyes glittered at me fiercely for a second and he clenched his effeminate hands. "Cribbed? Nonsense! What else? What else?"

So I told him. And what a second-hand shop it is! The concept of the Word of God, filched from us Greeks; the Eucharist, copied from the rites of Mithras; the resurrection, borrowed from half a dozen oriental godlings, *et cetera, et cetera*. I've even heard a rumour that the Nazarene's birth is celebrated on December 25th, birthday of the sun god in half the old religions of the East.

The bishop's face showed only a pulpy irritation. What a little man it is who is incapable of doubt!

So I finished with the virgin birth, stale as the world. What is so disgusting about copulation, I wonder, that gods may not be born of it? Countless centuries ago the Egyptian goddess Neith gave virgin birth to the sun; Isis to Horus, Nana to Attis. Io was made pregnant by a hand, Danae by sunlight. We have more recent legends of Plato, Alexander, Caesar Augustus. And only last May some gabbling Jew informed me that Hannah was impregnated by an invisible penis (poor lady!) to give virgin birth to Samuel.

The bishop of course had excuses for this. For a while, without hearing a word, I watched the rosy bud of his mouth opening and closing, then my gaze detached itself round the room. In front of me a huge wall-fresco showed the myth of Perseus and the Medusa whose hair – a myriad sleek-eyed snakes – resembled a city council in debate. The councillors themselves were trying to be agreeable. Some of them had brought their wives, and the hall stank of fenugreek. Tetricus had fallen asleep. The Master of the Offices was tasting damsons and kept dabbing his mouth fastidiously with a napkin.

I noticed that the Augustus was regarding us with interest. His quick ears, I suppose, had detected something the bishop had said, while I had been oblivious. And now he called across to us: "What is it you say, bishop? That the soul is evil?"

The whole room fell quiet. I heard the faint snoring of Tetricus. The bishop said unabashed: "Pardon me, Augustus, the soul of man is corrupt from birth."

Constantine demanded with his soldier's bluntness: "Then how can he find God? Would sin not make God go away?"

The bishop had stood up in respect. "Only if the sin is unrepented, sir," he said. "As men we are certain to sin. We sin in everything. In our words, in our thoughts, even in our love. The Augustus will forgive me."

Constantine was frowning and staring. I know that intense look. He gives it when something rankles. The Empress reclined very cool beside him, sipping wine. He said: "Then how can a man get the support of God? How does he know if he has not driven God away by some sin?"

"A man must have faith," the bishop said.

The Augustus looked perplexed. "What do you say, Synesius?"

I too stood up, irked to be involved in this farce and glad that there was probably no educated man in the room. I said: "The corruption of the soul is a myth of the Galileans, Augustus. As for faith, the virtue of that must depend on what a man has faith in. The Manichees have faith in the Devil. The Germans have faith in their bloodthirsty and ridiculous gods. Faith is nothing without reason. If men had lived by it they would never have smelted iron or even ploughed a field."

The bishop now went into a most unbalanced diatribe against reason. The man has no more idea of metaphysics than my mule. All the time we were speaking the Augustus was frowning and moving his jaw about, which meant that all the city councillors did the same. I've never seen so many people masticating on nothing. Only the Empress looked slightly contemptuous, but of who or what I could not tell. She often does. At the end of the bishop's speech the Augustus merely said: "So the soul is rooted in evil?"

The bishop bowed, and the Augustus returned to his duck stew with a look of preoccupation. The councillors also managed to look preoccupied, and ate duck stew, and slowly the guests warmed themselves back into conversation, like bullfrogs waking up in the Pontine marshes.

The drinking part of the evening was interminable, and I had to endure the sight of the bishop's jowls garlanded in autumn roses. The twinkle of forgiveness in his sweaty little eyes was more than I could bear. Before we left I felt under the couch, picked up a duck bone and presented it to him. This was not well done, and I regret it. He asked me, of course, what this was for, and I said I understood that the Christians worshipped bones. He had the dignity not to reply. But it's certainly true that these people venerate the remains of their dead leaders – a revolting practice. I have myself seen crowds of Christians, men and women, kissing the supposed knee-pan of an apostle. My friend the physician Eutropius was with me, and said that in fact it was the knucklebone of a sheep.

As I think of the Augustus I marvel at the complexity of what we call intelligence. When he talks about God or philosophy he is like a blundering boy, and he is utterly ignorant of any history, science or logic. Yet presented with a practical situation he knows exactly what to do and within seconds will make decisions which would shatter me. While I am studying history, he is making it. It turns me into dross. Synesius, you old pedant!

IV

Hosius, Bishop of Cordoba, to the Bishop of Ipagrum in Spain.

22 September

YESTERDAY, dear brother in Christ, I had a chance to bear powerful witness to our Faith. In the retinue of the Augustus there's one man without religion. He is the Master of the secretariats, and although I do not detect that he has impeded any business of our own, he is a stumbling-block in the path of goodwill.

At Modena, during a great banquet, he openly challenged our scriptures. How wisely was it said by St. Paul that faith to the Greeks is foolishness! This Secretary – a sage only as far as the beard – cannot concede that the truth may be beautiful. His very appearance is petty – a strange little person who often wears a skull-cap to conceal his baldness. Similarly he wears reason to conceal his emptiness.

During the banquet the Augustus asked me about the corruption of the soul. It is clear that these things worry him, but alas his mind is little swayed by doctrine. He wishes to harness God to his purposes, instead of harnessing himself to God's. When I told him that the spirit is sinful from birth this was at once denied by the Secretary, who went on to speak very foolishly about the gift of faith, and to extol reason. All this, my brother, was perpetrated in a hall filled with the influential people of Modena. I wept inwardly for my Christ.

But the Augustus is gracious, and he allowed me to answer. With God's help I spoke fearlessly what I believe. Reason, I said, is the last citadel of the poor in heart. We do not love with our reasons, we don't pray or forgive with them. All the tender moments of our lives – the people we embrace, the memories we cherish, the beauty which elates us – none of these is fed by reason. They belong to the holiness of experience.

The mind, I said, is the servant of experience, not experience of the mind. How does a child first reason? He touches a blade and is cut. So he knows that a knife is harmful. He strokes cat's fur and he laughs. He knows that the coats of cats are soft. Precisely so do we come to be sure of God in our hearts.

As for reason, it constantly changes. Was it not evident to our ancestors that the seas fell over the edge of the world? But today we are not sure. Such intellect has betrayed man always. But God, never. It is He, after all, who created our brains. How monstrous, then, if with our brains we try to unseat Him!

It is my belief that whatever he may think, the behaviour of man is not rooted in logic, but springs from a hidden web of desires and aversions. These he gilds with the fair meanings of his mind, which is no more than a laying of ashes over chaos. How often have we not heard of the most grave and rational of men, who are Pythagorean by day, but Dionysian by night?

And all the time God is speaking to our souls.

V

Commonplace Book of Synesius.

ONCE again astride the infernal mule. But our march is easy and all the bridges are standing except for one over the Rhenus which had been downed not by soldiers, but by the diligent citizens of Bologna. Our advance engineers had commandeered barges and thrown a makeshift causeway across before we arrived. Bologna itself opened its gates and it seems now that all the cities of Cisalpina are ours.

Yesterday I attended the Augustus at a vital meeting of the commanders. The issue: where do we cross the Apennines? But it was clear to me that Constantine had already made up his mind, and now had only to make up those of his generals. Of these the leader of the German auxiliaries was consulted only from diplomacy, and spent his time running his great stubbled finger over the maps in fascination. Sacrovir insisted that we plunge southward into the mountains by an obscure pass from Faventia. His fair rat's face flushed and sparked at any opposition. He is the kind of man who interprets all criticism as personal hostility, and I noticed that even the Augustus went warily with him. But it was a flamboyant plan, needlessly dangerous. The road was known to be steep and falling into decay, and Constantine eventually silenced him by pointing out that his own cavalry would be at a heavy disadvantage there.

The Marshal, who rarely speaks, became almost eloquent about our taking the main pass from Bologna to Florentia, and Tetricus cautiously supported him. Here the Augustus pointed out the dangers of committing the army so early to a long and irrevocable line of attack through mountains. Tetricus grudgingly assented, while the gaunt Marshal withdrew into his silence.

Constantine and Geta favoured a rapid march down the Via Flaminia, the finest road in the country, which moves inland across Umbria and so exposes us to the Apennines for as short a time as possible. This way our purpose would remain uncertain until a late moment. Geta wanted to leave the great road suddenly and cut across the mountains by Lake Trasimene as Hannibal had done. But Constantine overruled him; the track was rough and would quickly dissipate the advantage of our speed. Observing this slight, watchful Geta, I imagine his cleverness is typical of a planner who has experienced few of the practical difficulties of fighting.

Constantine enjoyed this meeting, I could tell. He likes encountering men's real minds and wills instead of their sycophancy. He also likes to win. I think too that the swiftness of the march appeals to him, because he now wants to force matters to their end. Only the bandy-legged Sacrovir was dissatisfied. He remained behind after the rest had gone and said: "We could fight a great campaign here, Augustus, a dazzling campaign! We could round up these Italians like chickens." He spoke as if it was a game of backgammon.

The Augustus still keeps me up at barbarian hours of the night. Wherever we camp — around an inn, a post-house or a village — he sets up makeshift headquarters where the legionary prefects report and his staff discusses the day's progress. The Empress camps nearby and sleeps in a small but luxurious tent, or even in her carriage. It does not occur to the Augustus that there are men in the army less inured to hardship than him. He can ride for twelve hours and look fresh in the evening.

It is the night torture in his mind which undoes the day. But his generals never see it. It is I — fourteen years older than Tetricus — who still limp into the middle hours of darkness writing orders and confidential letters until my eyelids are clanging shut. He rarely dictates his journal to me now, it has become too personal. And he no longer strides about, but sits in a chair, gripping its sides to hold himself quiet.

The scars in him are more raw than ever. Last night he dictated orders to me for so long that the lamp suddenly went out and we were left in darkness. I heard him blundering about the room among chairs and chests, and his voice as he shouted for light was a mixture of threat and panic. Cecrops came at once with a lantern. I think this old man did not realise I was in the room, and I saw a strange thing: he patted the Augustus' cheek as if he were a child, and said: "No, no, Gaioo, it's only the day with its eyes closed." The odd, sing-song voice he used made it sound like a nursery-rhyme, and I remembered that this dog-like creature has served Constantine since infancy. The Augustus seemed unaware of the peculiarity of this scene, and went on dictating as before, while the rustle of Cecrops' sheepskin coat sounded on the far side of the door as he curled back to sleep.

It must be this false equilibrium in Constantine which deludes me that the army, instead of marching over plains, is teetering along the spine of a mountain, where a little breeze could blow it into the abyss.

Today we were moving south again. Ever since Modena we have been skirting the Apennines but not seen them for mist. Around us the fields are full of yellowing vines whose grapes are gone. The land is well farmed, but already depopulating. Taxation bears so heavy that people cannot afford children, and infant mortality is high. In another generation even this wealthy province will be starting to decay. It is not difficult to guess where it will end, and the process is irreversible. We shall not again see the days of those yeomen farmers, fibre of the legions, who made this land the finest in the world.

That is the tragedy of our invasion. It is like an omen. Because these are the new masters – Gauls, Germans, Britons – coarsened in another climate, without the finer senses. Such men have all the qualities of war, but none of peace. They are chilling because one cannot know in what manner they feel. Their winter eyes betray no nimbleness of mind or heart. This can be sensed even in the long, arrogant stride of their march.

Constantine moves continually between the army's head and rear, exposing himself to whatever danger there may be. Such gestures, I suppose, inspire the loyalty of the unimaginative. In the centre of the column our court is reduced to a sliver. On today's march I noticed the Master of Latin Letters asleep in a wagon full of millet, like any farmer. But he fares better than I do. My mule is triple-jointed and can bite and kick me at will. Twice I have been jostled near the Bishop of Unctuous, and have had to feign short-sightedness. My mule bit his.

I must be getting old and timid, because there is something about that bishop which disturbs me more than the Gallic legionaries do. If his Christianity ever attained power it would persecute with a terrible vengeance. Like any other tyranny, it offers peace only at the price of submission. And what is so certainly true that one may submit to it? Certainty is death. Change is life. With this banality I end my day.

VI

Geta, Master of the Offices, to
Constantine Augustus.

Faventia, 26 September

REPORT on intercepted messenger: it is with deepest apology and regret, Eternity, that I must report the death of a messenger of the Empress on the Aemilian road near Placentia. This man refused to say from where he came or to submit to search. In the course of arrest he was mistakenly killed. I have ordered those responsible to be suspended and charged; but it seems that only after his death did it become apparent that he was a servant of the Empress. Herewith I send you the letter; its destination was Nice; and I again submit to your Eternity and to the Noble Empress my profoundest apology.

[The intercepted letter is not extant. It is presumed to have been destroyed by Constantine.]

VII

Journal-Memoir of Constantine.

Faventia, 26 September

I WILL record it now, before a sentence or feeling is lost. If words could embody the misery I feel, this page would turn to wormwood. I will never again delude myself about what is in me and what is in Fausta. These words will be a wall against lies. Always. Whenever I read them, may they scour out all the madness and creeping dreams in me. Even if they still fill me with grief, I'll be cleaned.

This is what happened. Late in the evening, while I was dictating to Synesius in the villa where we are camped, an orderly from the Master of the Offices arrived with a letter from the Empress to her cousin, apprehended in error on its way to Nice. Its seal was broken. I sat at the atrium table and read it, as I read all letters sent on from the Offices. At first I imagined it was my tiredness which made the letter sound so cold in all it said about me, but as I read on I realised this was not so. It made such a mockery of me that I felt as if ice were creeping along my veins. When I got up I experienced an odd, stiff weakness. My feet moved beneath me of their own accord, far down. I went to the outer door and told the tribune of my guard to fetch the Empress. Then I sat down, drew the table-lantern closer, and read it again. With every reading it grew colder, harder and less explicable. I did not recognise the woman who had written it nor the man about whom it was written. It spoke of me as tiresome to her, sometimes stupid. Her cousin was lending her a villa east of Rome, to spare her the tedium of accompanying me at the siege. In no phrase or word sounded any tone of liking, let alone of love. Although the night was still warm, I began to shiver. But my cheeks blushed. I held the letter away from me, kneading its parchment in my fingers as if the outlandish thing might vanish. But its reality was irrefutable. I had eavesdropped on Fausta's heart, if that is what it can be called. Its truth was as certain as if I'd read her diary, or overheard her confession in a temple.

She came alone, and the outer door closed behind her. Carelessly she hung her cloak over a lamp-stand. I watched her from the far side of the atrium pool, as I might watch a person a long way away. She wore a wide-sleeved, turquoise dress. She came towards me rather coolly. When she spoke she used that formal, self-possessed tone which at once filled me with rage. "Is anything wrong?"

I held the letter under her eyes. I was incapable of speech. She glanced at me, took it uncertainly and started to read. Soon the letter began to tremble in her hands, and her face tautened. Twice her gaze half lifted to mine, but fell back to the parchment. Then she laid it on the table and looked at me. "It's mine." She said the words with suppressed fear and a hint of defiance.

"I know it's yours!" My words came in a rushed whisper. "How dare you say 'It's mine' as if it was a wardrobe list!"

She still looked me in the face. "I didn't know your spies collected my letters."

"They don't." My voice refused to lift above a whisper. The terrible roar of it was trapped somewhere in my chest, under the breastplate. "Some half-wit servant of yours got himself killed on the road near Placentia." Even my whisper was choking.

"Why don't you use the imperial messenger service? I know why you don't. So you can write about me as you please. Where else do your messengers go? To Rome?"

"I write only to my cousin." Fausta's pallor was not quite her own; it was the colour of stone. "I don't expect my servants to be molested by yours."

"He was killed because he never showed your warrant! Perhaps he knew the filth he was carrying!" I snatched the letter from the table. "Have you read all this?"

"Yes."

"And nothing in it surprises you? Are all your letters stiff with this unfeeling?"

"I write to my cousin every week."

"And every week a betrayal!" My voice broke from its whisper into strangled shouts. "You speak of me as if I was a servant! No! Not even a servant! An irritation, an object of contempt! Look here —" I scanned the letter. "Listen: 'He will talk so about sacredness and truth, as if he could marshal them into line like troops.' By the gods, Fausta, do you feel that? Am I a quarter-brained philosopher, then? 'Sometimes he seems such a boy.' May those words suffocate! What am I to you then? What am I?" I flung the letter at her face. "So you accept a villa in some pleasure-resort for the winter! You don't wish to undergo the boredom of a siege with me. Is that right?"

"It seemed sensible. I could only be a liability to you."

"Liability!" The roar of my voice filled the atrium. "I agree, I agree! You're as trustworthy as a snake! No, Fausta, you'll not go to a villa. You'll stay by me. And if you stray beyond your guards, I'll have them drag you back by the hair!"

Her face was transformed by a fierce resentment. "You prove my letter now, Gaius. You're as stupid as I say."

I watched the change in her. It was like a ghastly triumph for me. "That's your real voice. Yes. That's the woman who wrote the letter."

She turned her back on me. "I can't change what I feel."

I noticed the slight quivering of her shoulders. I was tempted to wrench her towards me, but loathed to touch her. I said: "Feel? You're incapable of feeling." My voice filled with an appalled bitterness. "You're cold as winter. You hate men. You never speak of one without despisal."

She turned on me, blazing. I've never seen her look like that. The expression of her face was redirected by a score of lines which emphasized her jaw and eyes. "Men!" Her voice came low and withering. "What is there to admire in men? Are women such poor things that you can buy their love with marriage? I was married to you for convenience of state! I was eighteen. I'd scarcely seen you before. Love! Love! I don't want to hear that word." She spat into the pool. "Why do you come to me at night with that secret smile of ownership? How I hate it, I hate it! I don't want to be owned. I want to be left alone! I want to be *whole*! I *am* alone." Her voice was trembling, touched by hysteria. "I want you to keep away! Keep away!" Her shoulders wrenched violently as if I was touching her. "You say you love me, but yours is no more love than a bull's."

Her revulsion was absurd to me. There was nothing I wanted less than to embrace that cold body. "I'll never touch you!" I shouted it like a curse. "I was merely bewitched! I've heard a viper can bewitch a man to love it. I believe that!" I thought of all the times, for years now, that she had teased me with her body, how she alternately ignited, deadened and twisted my desire so that half our nights were passed in a kind of helpless fire. For four years I had burnt around her while she mocked me. Love? I had only been maddened. No man could love such a woman. She only cast a reptile spell on him. As the reverberation of my voice faded in the atrium, I said: "I don't love you. I loathe you."

Fausta's face was still unrecognisable, changed by its rancour and by some new pain. She demanded: "You said you loved me. You said so. Did you lie? Why? Why?"

I've touched the woman in her, I thought; but it was a meaningless victory: I said. "So you demand my love but refuse to give your own." My voice was rising again, I could not stop it. "Because your allegiance is already given, isn't it? You don't belong to the present at all, you belong to the past and that unspeakable brother. I tell you, Fausta, I'll break Maxentius in my own hands!"

I think she tried to spit at me. "Like you broke my father!"

Just then some slight movement in the shadows made me stop. I imagined a rat or a snake. I walked forward and peered closer. To my astonishment I saw that Synesius was still sitting at his desk. I had taken his lantern to read Fausta's letter, and had forgotten to dismiss him. He was crouched low, his face ashen. Now he stumbled forward and kissed my hand over and over. Poor fellow, I don't know what he expected of me, he had heard such things. I don't even know what I expected of myself. I was shaken and bewildered. A great flood seemed to be dying out of me. I clasped his hand and tried to smile at him. "I forgot to dismiss you," I said. I led him to the door. He was shaking. I felt as if he took away with him our last hope of sanity. I must have seen in him some chance of help, because just before he left I called something out. I think I asked: "What? . . . What do you . . .?" And that was all.

He turned round. His stare passed from me to Fausta. But the anger had left her face too; it looked like a sad mask. He said: "Forgive me, Augustus, madam. I understand too little. I'm old. What is this word love? I don't always know what is meant. Augustus, madam, forgive me." And he closed the door.

[*Commonplace Book of Synesius:* . . . the first time the Augustus shouted at her I got to my feet in the darkness and murmured to be excused, but neither of them saw or heard. After that I lost my nerve. They had already said unforgivable things. I crouched low behind the desk. The door was beyond them, and I was trapped. I was sure that my shoes' shaking on the mosaic floor would betray me. When he at last heard me I thought he would break my head open; poor, abject old Synesius. And instead he tried to ask for my advice!

What could I say? It's a long time ago for me, but I recall that there's a unique anguish about discovering the failings of the one we thought perfect. The myth of perfection is a perilous one. It is built on confusion. Can the trouble be that only one word for love exists in Latin, where we Greeks resolve it into many? The simple Latin 'love' confounds sex even with charity. Are all the lofty heart-wrenchings of this intellectually absurd man due to the poverty of a word?

But I could scarcely express this at the time. My teeth were chattering. I almost ran out of the door. As I turned round to close it, I saw that the Augustus had extended his hand most pathetically to me. . . .]

We stood in the half-darkness, without looking at one another. She, I remember, remained perfectly still by the pool.

The top of her head was lit faintly from the opening above, which showed a rectangle of stars. I replaced the lantern on the table. I felt utterly cold, as if the pit of grief in me went down for ever and my voice and movements floated above it. But I had to see this horror to its end. If my marriage had been a body, I would have cut out every canker from it, even though it died.

I'm sure that the night had turned very cold. I wrapped my cloak around my neck. I could not stop shivering. Suddenly I felt as if the woman standing by the pool was not Fausta any more. Fausta was gone. This other person I did not love or hate. She was simply the mouthpiece by which I would rearrange my feelings. She would define the depth of the pit.

I stood in the lantern-light at the other side of the water, and looked at her. I suppose that less than ten feet separated us, but my voice seemed to be calling to somebody on the far slope of a valley. I said: "Be honest with me." It suddenly seemed a stupid thing to say to Fausta, even after the letter.

"Yes."

"Did you ever love me?"

She said: "Never. I was terrified. Always."

The words fell like stones: small, irretrievable. "Sometimes in bed," she added, in the same bell-like, impersonal voice, "my desire to keep myself apart was so strong that I felt I was floating, looking down on my own body, on both of us."

I turned from her, walked a few paces away, and stood facing the garden, which shone dimly through the columns of the peristyle. "You felt guilty," I said, "for sleeping with the man who drove your father to his death." (That is how I described myself. And that is the truth.)

"No, I never felt guilt. I used his death against you to excuse my coldness, and sometimes to blunt your passion. Passion has always frightened me. Any feeling which is very strong frightens me." She was looking at me without discernible expression. I wondered: was she challenging me to fling abuse at her, strike her? I even felt she wanted this. But there was no anger in me, only the icy tension. I had dared her to be honest, and she was so with lucidity, as if she had thought far more words than she had ever spoken. She went on: "Perhaps also I hear voices talking about me. Yes, I often do. 'She would not sleep with her father's murderer', they say. You see, I have no morality, Gaius. Not like you. I simply hear other people discussing me. That is my morality.'' 'Gaius' rang out at me with a bitter remoteness, as if it echoed from a time of innocence. I could not tell how much these things were costing her to say. ''As for my father,'' she went on, ''I loathed and was terrified of him. I remember him only as an enormous, shambling peasant, who delighted in his uncouthness. For months at a time I never saw him, never wanted to. He always called me 'little girl', as if he'd forgotten my name. And I never forgave him for marrying me to you.''

Her voice retained its quietness. I stared down. A nymph looked up at me from the mosaic floor. When Fausta again said ''Gaius?'' I felt as if she was addressing a man whose pride had gone, who was thinned and fragile, almost nothing.

''Yes.''

''I've been as honest with you as I can.'' She came a few paces towards me. I met her gaze. She looked wracked and ill. ''You say you don't love me. What were your feelings then? Mine were nothing. But what were yours?''

The question frightened me. There are some easy ways of confessing, even to crimes. Joking or rage will conceal the horror of almost anything. But neither came to me. I wanted time. And I wanted, out of vanity, to ask her one more question. I said: ''I'll answer you. Only tell me: was there nothing in me attracted you?''

She said: ''I don't know. I'm not sure. I only know that your glory drugged me. Your command. Yes, Gaius, I loved your position, and mine beside you. I'm vain.'' She mocked herself. ''I felt like the empress of the universe enthroned beside you!''

''I thought perhaps you pitied me.''

''No, I spare you that.'' She laughed wretchedly, like a sob.

''You often gave me gifts.'' I don't remember if I felt any hope when I said this, or the tiniest warmth. I think not.

She said: ''The gifts were instead of love. They were a guilt-offering.'' She looked into the pool again. ''I'm sorry.''

We seemed like two ghosts, passionlessly tormenting one another. I peered vacantly about me. My gaze settled on the bust of an emperor in a niche: Marcus Aurelius. The villa's owner, I supposed, must claim him as an ancestor. The face was tilted back, and stared beyond us through melancholy eyes. In the marble beneath it was engraved: 'Awake from sleep, and realise all that troubled you were but dreams.' I looked at the blank face, as if to find its secret. Or was the man a fool?

Fausta said relentlessly: "You promised you'd answer me. What were your feelings?"

I stood close in front of her. "Why do you want to know?" I hoped to feel angry, but did not.

"I think I have a right." The skin of her face looked paper-thin over its bones.

I demanded: "Do you want to reduce me, as you've reduced yourself?" But again no anger came to me. Her eyes looked unnaturally dark and distended.

She said: "Tell me."

I hunted in my mind among things which I had never considered. My own fear surprised me. What had I felt for her? Why? Where did it spring from? She was gazing at me hard. It was true, she had a right to know. So I lifted my hand to the neck of her dress. She flinched. I pulled it down over her shoulders as I had once – a thousand years ago! – at Verona. I scarcely knew what I was going to speak. But I said: "You can't understand sensuality." She didn't answer. "A sensual man does not merely lust for a body, he dreams about parts of a body." My fingers travelled lightly over her shoulders. They moved as they might have moved over a map, without the faintest desire. Her skin felt cold, indifferent. I touched the valley under the collar-bone. "See there." I traced with my thumb the curve of rising flesh high above the corslet. "And there." Then I slid a hand under one breast, tilted it a little and pointed at the blue-veined skin. "And there." I lifted the dress back over her shoulders and said: "That, if you want to know, is what I desired."

She said: "And where's the wrong in that?"

"No wrong," I said, "but *that is all there is.*" My own words produced an unbearable tightness in my throat. There were doors opening inside me, opening on other rooms, on rooms I'd never dreamt of. I heard my voice go on: "I had a carnal fury to possess you, that was all. Not love. I wanted to consume you, totally. Can you understand? I could not bear your separateness. It maddened me." And now I heard myself say: "You would have destroyed this passion by loving me. If you'd loved me I'd have trampled on you, as I do everyone else, and thrown you away."

I stopped. I was filling with self-horror. Were these words true? I tried to grasp them. I said more slowly, searching: "If you'd been less cold I'd have been less fascinated by you. I admired your aloofness, because I had to contend against it. Yes, I adored the quality I hated." One by one the words as I spoke them created the facts. They became truth, and now stood irrevocable between us. "In any case, what's the use of it?" Bitterly I remembered the belief that union with earthly beauty foreshadows the Eternal. "It seems a pitiful way for a man to gain completion, doesn't it, that pumping in and out? Those gasps and moans? That wetness?" When I looked at Fausta now, she was ugly to me. The youthfulness had shrunk out of her. Her complexion seemed blotched, and I noticed the line of hair on her upper lip: a faint down where a sprinkle of sweat showed. "There's no completion." I looked away from her, up through the opening at the dim stars. "You wanted me to be honest."

She said: "I didn't want to preserve this passion in you. That's the irony."

"It's gone," I said. In her face I saw my own; it was torn and frozen. For the first time I considered that none of this might be our fault, but that we were the instruments of something else, and I felt a remote pity for her. In this dead calm we were speaking as if of other people, distant acquaintances. For some reason I imagined fish enclosed by some ornamental pond, turning and nudging one another in a subaqueous silence.

I stared at the wall-eyes of Marcus Aurelius. I wondered how Fausta and I would endure the future. I've heard it said that honesty binds people together. But I don't think this is so. I don't think we will face the knowledge of each other so simply, nor see our own poverty in one another's eyes without hatred. We are both too proud. We've stripped away too much flesh, and we'll have to cover ourselves again. What with?

I am aware that I have wanted to build a mystique about myself, as Diocletian did. Not a veil of incense and columns, but a god-like character. This mystique would be more self-deceiving than that of the old emperor. His was a decision of policy, mine arises from my vanity, my unease and a desire to touch the heavens. The trouble is that I am quite unused to talking or thinking about myself as I talk or think about other people. I've believed myself different.

What more, I wondered, did I owe to Fausta? One thing, perhaps. So I told her what I think now to be true: that my desire to eliminate Maxentius springs not only from his tyranny and his enmity to me, but from my own jealousy. "He bewitched you as I never could," I said. "Even now you're more a part of him than of me."

She was leaning against a column with one arm between her forehead and its stone. She seemed to have weakened at last. But she said distinctly: "I am more like him than like you, Gaius. Because neither he nor I was capable of love. We understood this in one another. We called it our demon's bond. We despised those who loved."

I felt futile in my hatred for Maxentius. I might kill him, but I could not destroy what he'd been. Fausta continued: "I've been frigid since childhood. I don't say this in self-pity. It's just a fact." She went on in a strange, shaking voice, with her face still hidden against her arm: "Did I tell you that I hoped you'd betray me for another woman? You see, I longed to love you." I stared at her in astonishment. "Yes, I thought that if you abandoned me I would feel − feel alive, jealous, wronged. It's terrible how I see myself in the eyes of others. Imagine it, the Empress wronged! But loving, loving, loving! Alive! That is what I wanted of you, Gaius, to love you more than I was loved." She was suddenly sobbing. "It must sound mad, after all I've said: but it's true. I dreamt of building my nobility, the depth of my feelings, out of your faithlessness." I could not see her face, but when she paused I heard her tears falling onto the stone floor. "It's too stupid even to be evil."

Why have I written this in such trembling, as if it was the unleashing of two souls? What have we said of one another? Nothing. Because there was nothing of us to remark, to value or to remember. Nothing, nothing. I have a false glory for her. She has a fine body for me. That is all. That is our souls, our passions, our five years of marriage.

That was our love.

VIII

Commonplace Book of Synesius.

YESTERDAY we approached a stream – a trickle at the bottom of steep banks – and crossed over by an old consular bridge, still firm and plain as Rome used to be. I asked the tribune near me: "What river is that?"

He replied: "The Rubicon."

So the ghost of Caesar strides before us into Umbria.

The same afternoon, we neared Rimini and the sun came out high and dazzling. As we approached the sea an extraordinary thing happened. Murmurs and shouts spread among the soldiers and several cohorts came to a complete halt. I realised that half these men had never seen the sea. An hour later they were swarming along it. Did it tip over the edge? Was that the end of the world? Some stood close to examine the little waves, then darted back when one broke, thinking the water was trying to bite them. Others threatened it with their spears. As for the Germans, awed into silence they thought it must be an enormous river, and started to sacrifice to it. Only the more experienced men, veterans from British days, were cleaning their armour in the sand.

Meanwhile, outside the yellow-stoned walls of Rimini, under a great arch dedicated to Augustus Caesar, a sycophantic prefect came forward with a speech. He compared Constantine to the divine seed entering Rome, his waiting bride. And he continued by likening Rome to Constantine's mother: a cruel mixing of metaphors. Incest is not among the Augustus' leanings. It was a revolting display.

Constantine isn't in the mood for unconscious humour. He wears his black, cold look. The prefecture of Rimini must have thought it was going to be slaughtered. But instead it was cursorily dismissed. Every act of the Augustus betrays a pent-up anguish. Two days ago he ordered me about with a glowering authority, to emphasise that the previous evening had never existed. Gossip, of course, is rife. His bellowing in the atrium that night even carried to the sentries of the Minervia legion. Yesterday evening he was covered in sweat while dictating field orders, even though the evenings are now cold. He sleeps alone.

The trouble is that like most people, even the very masculine, he is a natural worshipper. When he's shouting at the Empress about the villa or her coldness he's not shouting about that at all. He's saying: "Why are you not God? Where has your divinity gone?" He's angry with himself for being deceived by an idol.

As long as we regard anything as a gift from the gods, so long will it disappoint us.

I think that Constantine and the Empress loved what was worst in one another. A rude irony for the puritan Augustus. He, at first, was fascinated by her inaccessibility, which is no more than a cynical egotism. She admired his domineering and intolerance and, of course, his position. But his better part she despises or doesn't understand.

He notices none of this. In his mind he either lifts her to the stars or hurls her into hell. He cannot see she's just a frightened girl. No. He has to juggle with light and dark as if we were all part of an Egyptian mystery play. He's never noticed that there's no light, no darkness. It's all his dream. There's only a dusk, where people muddle about.

IX

Memoranda of Cecrops.

[about 29 September]

MAJESTY unwell three days. Stays up late, broods. This brings on the fever. Generals come with nonsense questions. Try to prevent. German prefect warded [sent off?].

Night-sweats and demon-talk. Last night writhing in his bed, wakes up and shouts Fausta. Early morning: red lines down Majesty's forehead to his eyes, inflamed. Apply flax with ox-dung.

Nights cold now. Dew. Bad for the back kidneys. Told Majesty to keep midriff wrapped in a long towel. Drink wine and honey, warm. Sleep on back.

No woman's worth a tear, say I.

X

Fausta to Marina at Nice.

[This letter was written in milk, invisibly. The recipient had sprinkled coal dust on it to reveal the words.]

30 September

IT is sad to be writing to you secretly, dear Marina, but necessary. The servant who brings this has another, formal letter which he carries openly. The reason for this subterfuge is that one of my slaves – a trustworthy but stupid man – was despatched with a letter to you ten days ago from Modena. He was intercepted and killed by agents of the Offices, and the letter was returned to Gaius, who read it.

I've written harder and more caustic things to you, Mari, than appeared in that rather innocent message, but Gaius' fury was terrible. He's already gaunt with strain, and this, matched by his raging eyes and uncontrolled mouth, made him look a little mad. In my own defence I lost my temper too. I expect we looked as crazed as one another. He fumed about the winter villa you offered me at Otricolum – I must refuse it now, dear cousin – and soon we were saying things which neither of us will forget.

It was frightening how we both stood there, Marina, like statues of ourselves in some haunted forum. I would not have cared if he had strangled me. There were even moments when I wished it. Never again will I be able to look into an atrium pool by night and feel at ease. It reflected the sky through the opening above, and was filled with shadows wrinkling among lost stars. It seemed to contain our madness. That, I remember thinking, was what the entrance to Hades must be. And I then believed – yes, I now believe – that one day Gaius will kill me.

I don't know how long we went on torturing ourselves and one another. Hour after hour it seemed, while the hopeless words came flopping out of us like toads on to the floor. He was as frank with me as I with him. He said he desired me only for a part of my body. He indicated the rise of my breasts, fingering them like a bored sculptor. Could there be anything more apparently humiliating than that? Yet here's a folly, cousin: this particular passion of his fills me with an animal pride. I used to be afraid that my breasts were too small.

116

But Gaius, of course, despises this love of his. At heart he's a prude. He called it 'carnal' – a word which derives from an older Latin, and which excludes the esteem of the mind and of the heart.

Marina, Marina, I think the gods have made us so that we must mock ourselves! We are all keys without locks, locks without keys! Gaius told me that my fear of his sexuality had only increased it. Isn't that heartless? If I'd loved him, I would have destroyed it. And listen to this: all these years his passion has disturbed and frightened me, and I've longed for it to be gone. But when that night he said "It's gone", it tore my heart. When I looked at him I saw my own radiance dying in his eyes. Don't smile. I can't put it any other way than that. I realised that I was no longer there in him. He watched me as disinterestedly as when we were first married. And I, who have always said I despised his love, felt uglier and littler for its absence. Tell me, Mari, am I alone in thinking we humans are most cruelly made?

I can't remember much more of what we said, although we talked about my brother, of course. You will not remember, but by Lake Verbanus there was a copse where lovers came. Maxi and I would crouch in the hollows of the oaks and wait until these couples lay together. We always laughed at people who loved, as if they had a disfiguring disease. We'd throw down sticks and acorns so they thought the place bedevilled. Children's games, you will think, but that's what we always felt about love, as if we had been born in disillusion. Even in our young adulthood neither of us had changed.

I remembered these things while Gaius was talking. Perhaps I exaggerate them. They are all confused in my mind now by that atrium pool full of drowning stars. Sometimes I've longed to be different. I told Gaius this. I grew very weak. I was not coherent, and I won't tell you any more. You tell me so little of your life. 'Lucullus had a long day at the law courts', you say. Or 'we picnicked at Alba'. Is it really all so placid? (You need not answer this. We wretched ones can never credit the happiness of others.)

Mari, I'm so old! The lines are already crawling round my eyes. Are there many women of twenty-four, do you suppose, who feel that their lives are over?

XI

Graffito written on the Flaminian road two miles from Fanum by legionaries of the Minervia.

[This verse, whose ribald tone partly escapes translation, continued to be sung by the soldiers of the northern Empire for many years after its context had been forgotten.]

> Imperial civil war is folly.
> Either her forces refuse to surround him
> Haw-haw
> Or he will not drive a wedge between her
> Haw-haw-haw
> The out-come is a come-out.

XII

Livilla Politta to Lucia Balba at Turin.

Forum Sempronii, 3 October

THINGS have been perfectly *dreadful* since I wrote. I feel I've aged a century. We've left behind half our wardrobe in Verona, and are now being jolted to pieces in the Apennines. If we stop we get rammed by a stone-throwing machine behind us – a huge spoon on wheels – and if we go too fast we become muddled in with the court baggage, which stinks of bad cooking. And this Flaminian road is meant to be the pride of Italy! When I complained of it to the tribune of our guard he said: "It was restored by the great Augustus Caesar, madam." As if that helped. The great Augustus Caesar has been dead these three centuries. Even by night we have no peace. We're reduced to sleeping in the most sordid places, with the armourers clashing and the trumpets of the watch echoing through the valleys every hour.

It's been the strangest week. Five days ago we reached the coast, then moved on to a town called Fanum Fortunae, which I feel is the last civilised place I shall ever see. The tribune escorted us round – to stop us going to the sea, I think, where the legionaries were doing peculiar things. The townspeople all knelt or prostrated themselves wherever we went – it gave me the weirdest feeling – while the tribune pointed out buildings in the Vitruvian style, whatever that is.

The next day, before I knew what was happening, we were into the foothills. They rise in tiers, with the higher Apennines behind. At first they were farmed, but now they're heavily forested, and frightening. The sun has gone and long clouds are rolling about the mountains. Apparently we're approaching a terrible pass, sheer on both sides, and our scouts are uncertain if it's defended. The Empress doesn't care a bit, and the servants are too silly to think anything.

The worst of it is that we don't hear the news any more, because the Augustus and she have had a frightful row. For all we know the army might be surrounded. I never look out without expecting to see armour glinting in the forests. The Empress is deathly pale and scarcely speaks. You'd think I wasn't there. I ask you, Biji, what's the point of a companion if you don't confide in her? But all she ever does is make unreasonable remarks. Yesterday she suddenly asked me if I'd loved my dear Cornelius. "I don't mean love your own feelings or the idea of marriage," she said, "I mean did you love *him*?" How could she ask such a thing?

This afternoon, when she was looking out of the window, I'm sure she was weeping. Her shoulders were shaking slightly, and she kept touching her cheek with the back of her hand. I never heard this argument of theirs, but half the court camp did. Apparently the Augustus thundered like Jupiter, then they were quiet and nobody heard any more. He called her a snake and a liability and a man-hater – I'm not sure how they're all connected – and finally asked her if she thought him some quarter-brained philosopher. Oh Biji, what a temptation!

Anyway, she's now rude to everyone, not just to me. When the Master of the Offices rode by and paid the usual respects, she demanded why he was smiling. He's the kind of little man who always smiles. So he had to pay his respects all over again, looking gloomy. Constantine sees her only once a day, very briefly and coolly. This morning he overtook our carriage with his staff – Wart-face, Bandy-legs and the rest – and merely said to her: "The army is entering the mountains, madam," as if we were blind. It's all too annoying. And I gather that the legionaries are singing the most disgusting things. I can't think why nobody stops them. But apparently it's a custom, so I suppose it's all right.

XIII

Journal-Memoir of Constantine.

152nd Mile-Post, Via Flaminia, 5 October

A FEW mornings ago Tetricus reported to me very angry, with his cloak torn at the shoulder. Our headquarters had been set up in an inn for the night, and my servant Cecrops had threatened him as he approached the gates and had tried to push him back with much abuse. I summoned Cecrops and dismissed him from my service. There could be no previous occasion, I raged, in which a praetorian prefect had been manhandled by a servant.

The result of this was pitiful. The old man fell at my feet and rubbed his white head against my sandals, sobbing for pardon. He had been upset, he said, at the way the generals disturbed my peace (peace!) and a black demon had led him to grab at the prefect. I remembered all the years Cecrops had served me, ever since my childhood at Sirmium, carrying my armour through five German campaigns. Something ached in my chest. I lifted him up and kissed him. At that moment I would have dismissed my army rather than him.

The sadder I am, the more greatly childhood memories disturb me. This morning, as we marched towards the great pass of Intercisa, my parents came into my mind with a piercing clarity, walking together through their farm in Dardania. It's one of those memories, unremarkable in itself, which the mind has inexplicably retained, and I saw them again as if they went in front of us, she already stout and slow, he bluff and soldierly. It was my mother who used to say that love is poured down by the gods (although she never explained how she knew) and sometimes as a boy I used to look at them, my mother and my father, and think how peculiar it was. I supposed they had some secret at night, because during the day they ignored one another. And when I was thirteen they were suddenly divorced, so that my father could marry into the purple. I've never asked my mother if the gods approved.

'Love.' I think I do not want to hear this word again. It came most quickly to my lips, I now realise, when they were pressed against Fausta's bosom. It was gasped, not spoken. *I love you.* I call on my own soul to listen to me: that in this figment 'love' I hid possessiveness, lust, and the desire to conquer. Was this the yearning of the spirit for purity? Did I seek Eternity in its earthly image? How laughable! This Eros, whom Plato said incited souls to heaven, can no more transfigure us than a horse can. He merely carries us, with our faults undimmed, into another country; we imagine that we do not know it, but in fact it is an old, familiar landscape: it, too, is ourselves.

The bishop once told me that love covers many sins, and I think the Christians are right when they say that the spirit is sinful from birth. This answers to my own experience. I am tired of accepting things which do not so answer. Plotinus, for instance, declares: 'Love is the act of a soul seeking God.' Is that what I feel? No. Cecrops says love is a penis.

But I no longer hate Fausta. I've been angry with her long enough for not joining in this farce. I did her wrong. She was clearer-minded than me, and was right to call me a boy. But we go warily with each other now. We will have to rediscover what we are. I imagine integrity as a quality of light: a kind of grey translucence, sunless. It is not at all beautiful. But it makes other lights seem disfiguring. Sometimes I imagine that Fausta and I look at one another across this wilderness, without the consolation of our lies, as if we were at the edge of the world. It seems childish to hope for brighter colours.

A curious effect of our indifference was that when I thought of Maxentius this morning I felt no hatred at all. I even had a desire to talk with him. Like me, I thought, he'd understand the loneliness of rulers.

It was at this foolish moment, while we rode towards the pass, that one of Geta's orderlies brought news from Rome: infants disembowelled and offered to Hecate, officials set to work in graveyards to dig up bones for curses and amulets. This woke me. Fausta's brother. The same darkening came over my eyesight as once before, but this time fleetingly. I recalled the old curse 'Hecate closes out the light'. I think this was because Fausta once told me how she and Maxentius used to bandy it about. And now I could not erase it from my mind. It throbbed in my temples like a lump I could touch.

This throbbing increased as we neared the Intercisa. I think I was a little feverish. Places don't normally affect me, but this was no normal place. The light seemed strange. All morning clouds had covered the peaks, and the sun had vanished. The slopes around us were matted with a dark or yellowing forest, the roadsides overgrown. We went among wild fig-trees and ivy-smothered pines. Tetricus' horse tried to bolt.

The mountains lifted before us in such a barrier that only the steady climb of the road made a pass imaginable. The enemy, I knew, was not defending it; but my temples went on pounding, and I thought how no god protected us. Far down on our left the river Metaurus was brimming and green. Above us the cliffs rose for two hundred feet, black with clouds so we could not see their summits. We entered the gorge. Our horses were rolling their eyes and sweating with fear. My own hands felt clammy on the reins. Before us the defile extended in gate after gate of sheer rock, as if these were the portals of the Styx. Soon the whole head of the army was engulfed in it. For half a mile we were marching at the bottom of a chasm. The only sound was the clash of our harness. I thought of Maxentius and wondered why he had not defended such a pass. It seemed given up to demons and the river. Geta said uneasily: "Our scouts are still watching the fort beyond the gorge. But the enemy's not moving."

We entered the tunnel cut by the Emperor Vespasian two and a half centuries ago. His carved inscription still showed above it. For a moment the noise of our armour was enough to waken Hades. The next moment we were out.

The enemy fort did nothing. It neither attacked nor sent anyone to make terms. I despatched a tribune and some men, and they were received by an old centurion unsure what to do. An hour later he relinquished the pass to us without bloodshed.

As we descended Vespasian's cutting, I felt as if we'd already crossed the summit of the Apennines. But this isn't so. In front of us rolls an ocean of wooded hills. The scouts who come in say that the country is deserted for more than a hundred stadia ahead of us. What is Maxentius doing?

All day I was conscious of marching along the same road as Vespasian took against his rival in Rome. I am attacking a dog, while he was attacking a pig [an allusion to the gourmand Emperor Vitellius] and I pray to whatever deity is listening that our outcome will be the same. He was victorious.

I've heard it said that on his deathbed the blunt emperor joked that he was turning into a god. And sure enough, the senate voted to deify him. That soldierly humour was sensible. But it hasn't been emulated in our time. The emperors of our age have inclined to believe in their divinity.

Yet I myself remember enough of these gods! – the artificer Diocletian, who stunted my advancement as a youth; Fausta's father, a dissolute schemer; Maxentius himself; and the Caesar Galerius, who hated me and whom I hated. Him in particular I remember, with his pitted jaws and livid eyes, exposing me to dangers in battle. I picture him on campaign in Persia, squatted among rocks like an ape, picking the diseased skin between his toes. Was that a god? Yet he killed and imprisoned men – Christians mostly – who did not burn incense to him.

And I too. What of me? Fausta's is the only view of me of which I may be sure. Through her I eavesdrop on the opinion of the world. And she evidently despises my intellect and hates my bestiality. A strange god. These days, even if the sun shines, I rarely look up. I feel stifled. I'm no longer the regent of the God. Where is He, who is He? I've discovered myself, but lost Him. If it's true that sin is that which cuts us off from divinity, I must have been deluded that He ever knew me. This whole campaign – more than forty thousand men – is launched merely on my vanity. We march in a spiritual darkness. Little wonder I no longer look my soldiers in the eyes.

XIV

Geta, Master of the Offices, to Constantine.

6 October

THIRD report of this month from Rome:

On 30 September crowds in the circus openly taunted the tyrant and proclaimed the goodness and invincibility of the Augustus. Graffiti lauding the Augustus are now prominent all over the Subura and the forums.

The honorary chariot races have been announced for 26 October. Further riots are anticipated.

Spies probing the loyalty of the Praetorian Guard to the tyrant: no report.

Attached: a list of new elements recruited to the enemy: their arms, experience, names of commanders.

May the Augustus live for ever.

XV

Journal-Memoir of Constantine.

Suilla, 8 October

FOR the last three days we've moved among wooded hills. The road has been overlooked from many sides and it's impossible that our advance has not been detected. For twenty miles the way followed the Metaurus valley, the river a mere trickle, and wound in and out of passes shaley with erosion. There were signs of viniculture here, but the farmers have long since gone. For an hour a day I've been riding with the court secretariats, receiving petitions and complaints. There's a restful domesticity about settling the stipends for junior clerks when we may all be dead in a week.

After Luceoli the road left the river and lifted among grey boulders. Sometimes I saw my legions coiled below and was gripped again by dread at our defencelessness.

[Here follow sketches and notes on infantry formations most effective for the defence of wooded inclines.]

We entered the clouds. This afternoon they were so thick that I could see no farther than my own retinue. Synesius made learned allusions to *The Clouds* of Aristophanes. He inhabits a strange world. Wherever we are, he is somewhere else.

For a while I stood on a knoll with the Bishop of Cordoba, but the sight of the spear-tips in the haze below unsettled me. They looked not only threatened, but drowned. I told my standard and tribunes to precede me on the road, and the bishop and I rode out of sight of the army and talked for a few minutes. I took the opportunity of asking him about the Christians martyred under Diocletian and Galerius, and he told me, with a wary respect, that there could only be One God, and that not all the emperors had been his servants. I heartily agreed. It is sad what a perilous world these Christians live in. But when he started talking about the Christian god, I could not grasp whether there was one of him or three. Five minutes listening to doctrine, and even my horse is asleep.

I asked: "This Jesus of yours, did he marry?" I sometimes think Fausta literally haunts me.

"No, Augustus."

I looked at his genial face, and wondered how much of my anguish was known to the court. I said: "It was you who told me that love covers many sins. Do you remember?" He inclined his head. "What do your gospels say about women?"

I noticed that his expression at once grew hot, almost angry. "They say, Augustus, that *those who touch women shall have trouble in the flesh.*" He flushed and went on: "They say that it's better to marry than to burn in hell, Eternity. But they exalt celibacy." His hands had dropped the reins of his mule and were clenched at his chest. "Augustus, in all the works of our fathers there is no commending word on sexual love."

These words filled me with an obscure peace. But this quiet did not transfer itself to him. His voice shook a little. "Women are a corruption of the mind, Eternity! They deflect the soul from its purpose." His neck quivered. "What is pure in love, Augustus, you will not find in that between men and women."

The new calm went on spreading through me. I closed my eyes in the sunlight. My horse grazed. The misery of the past two weeks had dulled in me, ready to erupt again, but for the moment eased away. The army's tramp and clinking were no louder than a stream on the other side of the knoll. The bishop subsided, afraid, I think, that he had alienated me. He said more composedly: "Even your Plato calls the body the tomb of the soul."

I answered to reassure him: "All you say is true, bishop."

I took off my helmet and rubbed my fingers through my hair. I felt surprised at my own peace. The clouds flooded to the horizon, and lapped at the hills under our feet. We looked towards Rome. The bishop seemed happy again and was beaming up at the sky as if it belonged to him. His confidence is contagious. This, I think, is why I can speak to him in depression. He will not accept and echo it, but meet it with optimism.

I said: "Have you ever looked down on clouds before, bishop?"

"Never, Eternity."

I pointed at one shaped like a cat. As we discussed it, it elongated to a crocodile.

"What miracles!" the bishop said. "Everything changing, reforming! The clouds make their own hills and valleys. What a greatness it is, Augustus! And will my lord look over there" – he pointed to a grey cluster. "What is it doing? It's bubbling like a pot! Who could look on such things and deny God?"

These suppurating clouds appeared to lie north of Rome. I don't know what kind of omen this was. I said: "The tyrant's committing new horrors."

The bishop replied formally: "My lord will be victorious."

I remembered the latest reports from Rome. I suppose I wanted the bishop's comfort. I said: "He's surrounded himself with Chaldean demon-worshippers and astrologers. Hosts of them. Do you know about such people?"

"They tamper with the underworld," the bishop said. "I knew them in Spain. But I was not afraid of them." He did not look afraid either. He was smiling. "Demons are only evil angels."

I stared into his round face. "Angels are stronger than men."

"But we have the cure for such evil, Augustus!" he answered ebulliently. "We are invulnerable!"

"How?"

For a moment he looked uneasy, then he edged his mule away from me a little and felt inside his robes. "With this!" he answered, and held something up. It flashed in the sun above me. I stared up at it. It was a large, silver cross. "Nothing can withstand this!" He was almost laughing with his certainty. "Not even demons which inhabit bodies! It tears them from their lairs, Augustus. It drives them even from shrines and statues!" He cradled the cross in his fat hands. I could not take my eyes from it.

But I said harshly: "What can your cross do to a tyrant? He's set people to dig in graveyards for amulets. Every hour he recites the Seven Vowels."

"Good, good, my lord! That means he's afraid!" Even his mule, as it shuffled and pawed, seemed to be dancing a little with the ecstasy of this extraordinary man. "Amulets! He's serving gods who've died, Eternity."

All the time he spoke he was fondling the cross. In the declining sun it glittered against his dark robes. "The tyrant has treated with demons for years," I said.

"Demons are not easily summoned," the bishop answered. "And when they come they're unpredictable. There were demons in my native city which turned and devoured their magician. Their only certain exorcism is by the cross." It lay still and shining in his hands now. It mesmerised me.

"Why then do you conceal it in your robes?" My voice sounded bullying in spite of myself.

"Some people are afraid of it, my lord," he said. "Godless people. Its power is known."

I noticed how low the sun was, and turned my horse. "You may wear it if you wish," I said.

XVI

Fausta to Marina at Nice.

[*about 9 October*]

I HAVE little to tell you, dear Mari, except of endless horizons. Every time we crest a hill or spur, there is another hill or spur before us – or twenty of them. But we are half way through the Apennines towards Rome, and other news of us may reach you before this does.

What can I say? I close myself in my carriage. The soldiers, apparently, are singing lewd songs. Livilla has tried to be kind. I must be a dull friend, and I think she's frightened.

Whenever we are moving, I open the window and look out at mountains. Sometimes gold and reddish shrubs show among the green on the hillsides, rather pretty. Today our tent was pitched by autumn crocuses of a kind you and I never found in Gaul: white, feathered with violet.

He comes occasionally to my carriage. We talk surrounded by his staff.

The road now goes through hills which are fearfully eroded. Rifts of flaking stone line some of them from top to bottom, and the valleys are full of torn-up trees. Our carriage wheels make an odd rustle on the polished stone. Several of the siege engines in front of us have broken down and were abandoned because of the speed of our march. I haven't seen a single inhabitant for three days.

But there was one moment of beauty which pierced even this heart. Four days ago we entered a great gorge. You've never seen such a place. On one side, a hundred feet below, the river wound over white rocks. On the other the slopes lifted into fearful precipices. We went like mice high above the water along the flank of the cliff, which was streaked with black as if the stone were weeping. The clash of our armour was frightful. Livilla grew scared and closed her window. You could feel the nervous dancing of our horses on the rock floor. But I went on looking out.

And suddenly, as we rounded a corner, the sun struck the cliffside beyond. It rose eerie and beautiful out of its shrubs, two hundred feet above us perhaps. Rooks were flying far up in the half-light, with the river green below.

It's terrible how I ache for something, anything, to lift me from my own littleness. And that, for a moment, is what this place achieved. How I long to feel the passion which Gaius has felt, and so despises! I wouldn't care if it was good or evil, provided it delivered me from my eternal self-control. Just once. Just for a day, an hour. I imagine your forehead frowning, Marina, and this isn't anything I expect you to understand.

Yesterday he talked for a little longer than usual. We looked dead into one another's eyes. Once we actually laughed at something together. But even our laughter sounded different, as if we were decorating with it, and our talk was about anything unimportant. We're like ancient children, playing together.

XVII

Synesius, Master of the Sacred Memory and private secretary of Constantine, to Geta, Master of the Offices.

10 October

THIS army being like a snake, with you at its head and I, unfortunately, in its belly, I take the liberty of sending my messenger to you.

You will have observed the unease of the Augustus, and will have recognised from what it springs. I would respectfully suggest the following:

1. That the more disturbing reports from Rome, especially those relating to the magic arts *et cetera* of the tyrant, be deferred for the time being, since they cannot bear practically on the decisions of the Augustus.

2. That reports on the health of the Empress, which is manifestly insecure, be forwarded to the Augustus by the imperial physician.

XVIII

Geta to Synesius.

[By return messenger]

THE interests of the state will not be served by averting our eyes from facts. Few men would agree with you that the magic practices of the tyrant may not bear on our circumstances. Nor is it my custom to suppress anything which His Eternity wishes to know.

The reports of the imperial physician do not fall within my department.

XIX

Commonplace Book of Synesius.

Mevania, 12 October

WE are ruled by madmen. Every officer in the army seems to
mutter protective gibberish, and now even Geta is infected.
The closer we draw to Rome the more bedevilled and bedemoned
we become. As for the priests, a mouse cannot squeak in the
Umbrian woods without its being ominously interpreted. Very
soon the motions of an eagle or a woodlouse will redirect the
whole campaign.

For several days we have marched through upland valleys,
lightly farmed for rye. Unlike the towns in the eastern Apennines,
which had been deserted in fear, these ones are surprised
altogether by our arrival, and their people cluster in the doorways
to watch us, with women and children unafraid. Our quartermaster has paid for the food and fodder requisitioned from
them – all through the valleys their barns are full – and the
Augustus deals sternly with any of our men found marauding,
and savagely with those convicted of rape.

Yesterday evening, while I was riding with the imperial staff,
we reached Forum Flaminii where the road bifurcates. The
townsmen lined the streets and stared at us curiously, not
knowing which the Emperor was and making no obeisance. I told
Constantine about the emperors slain here by the pretender
Aemilianus sixty years ago, and either because of this, or to
obtain an augury on the road, he made sacrifice. I was standing
close to him as he did so, and I observed how grim he looked.
He killed the offering himself, but his hand shook with the knife
and when he dedicated it he did not cry "To our Comrade, the
Sun Invincible" as he used, but simply said rather quietly: "To
the Great God." Nothing more.

This afternoon we reached Mevania and I saw again, for the
first time since my youth, the soft flood of the Clitumnus idling
through its trees. This is the river, sacred to our fathers, which
carries the merchandise of the plains in small boats to Rome.
So we have entered at last the watershed of the Tiber. The
whiteness of the cattle on the banks, some say, derives from the
purity of the waters by which they pasture – a pretty legend – and

130

I could not look at it without nostalgia. How many afternoons I remember, strolling among its cypresses as a student and talking philosophy with friends long dead! Plotinus, Porphyry, the New Cynics — such earnest, hopeful times! I could scarcely bear to witness our legionaries gouging out earthworks for their night camp all along the green glades. I'm becoming a sentimental old man. After all, what did that Neoplatonist talk amount to? Pretentious humbug!

To the perplexity of his staff and the panic of his physician, the Augustus plunged naked into the river's cold waters, and remained swimming for a long time. If this was done for cleanliness, I sympathise. The sweat of armoured men is appalling; you'd think our smell must precede us by fifty stadia, and vitiate any chances of surprise. But the Augustus could have cleaned himself better in the public baths of Mevania, as I did. No, I think his motive for immersing himself in these purifying waters was very different. I stood a little downriver from his staff, watching him, and he swam with a rapt preoccupation, not noticing their anxiety. When he moved close to me I saw that his eyes were closed, as if he were asleep. But as he came near the bank he suddenly looked up and demanded in his blunt way, as if we were talking in his tent: "Have you sent my message to the Empress?"

His face looked pared and unfamiliar below me, with its hair flattened and beard plastered against his cheeks. "I have, Eternity," I answered.

He grunted and swam away. What was in the grunt I don't know, but I think I heard relief. Every evening he sends her a curt enquiry after her health — a substitute for seeing her. Since I ride not far from the Empress' carriage, I've noticed how they never converse for more than five minutes. Once I was close enough to see his expression as he talked, and I thought he watched her with a kind of appalled fascination, as a man watches a snake. She has grown thinner and paler, and closes the window of the *carruca* whenever we halt. Sometimes I've glimpsed her before her tent is set up, pacing over the grass like a cat; but more likely one sees only the Lady Politta, mincing about with a depleted train of servants. It is clear to me now that the Augustus and the Empress, whatever they may believe, are fatally attached to one another. She, for some reason, has suppressed this. He has argued himself away from it. Theirs is the reciprocal yearning of two people utterly unlike. However much they rage or confess, they will always remain ignorant of one another, and such ignorance will be tinged with respect.

The Augustus climbed from the river with the same drugged movements as those of his swimming, and was rubbed down on the bank by slaves. It was now dusk. I walked among the trees, remembering foolish things, and enjoyed the sleek waters and the wakening stars. My own past used not to interest me, but nowadays I sometimes find myself speculating on it, as if it was somebody else's, and recall a young man named Synesius, who seems too ugly and pedantic to have been me. Forty years ago my friends called me 'Scorpion', because I was small, dry and stinging. I wonder: do we have no power to change ourselves at all? Sometimes in those days I wanted to fling my arms about and speak hugely and irresponsibly. (I would have been more attractive to women that way.) Why did I never do it?

I noticed lamps shining among the cypresses, and went quietly. Some thirty soldiers were squatting in a clearing. I thought I must have stumbled on a rite of Mithras, because the men were holding hands. Then I saw the Bishop of Cordoba sitting amongst them, cradling a loaf like a baby and beaming in his fatuous way as if this circle of half-wits was the senate of Rome. I did not care to approach nearer, but they were evidently starting one of their sacramental meals. I heard disconnected phrases chorused through the trees. ". . . For life and knowledge . . . slain for us . . . in remembrance. . . ." Just as the worshippers of Dionysus gnaw bulls' flesh hoping to imbibe the strength of Zeus, so do these Christians, with the followers of Attis and the rest, eat the flesh and drink the blood of their god to gain his strength. Doubtless, like all other gods, his blood will be sucked until he is withered and forgotten; but it pains me to think that our army brings nothing finer to Rome than these stagnant orientalisms.

As I walked back along the river I remembered the talk of the Divine and of Matter which my friends and I had exchanged so fervently along these banks. That talk, at least, sprang from free minds. We may have been pedants, but we were not slaves. For any rational man the truth of Christianity was long ago demolished by Porphyry. But then there are no rational men any more. They are all mystics and fools.

XX

Journal-Memoir of Constantine.

WE reached Mevania by early evening. The air was full of a presaging heaviness, and I made sacrifice. I could not tell what this atmosphere meant, only that it clustered thick about us and that the whole land was quiet. For the first time in many days we entered a town which had been abandoned. The noise of our marching intruded like a blasphemy, and I had the soldiers pitch camp beyond the walls.

I made a routine inspection of the bridge over the Clitumnus, and crossed back as the sun was falling. The sacred river glided among trees; even the cattle on the banks are white with its purity. As I looked, its surface darkened and shone, as if some hand were smoothing the waters in flowing circles of light. It was very tranquil.

I dismounted and immersed my arm. The waters writhed between my fingers, as if alive. I ordered Cecrops to unstrap my breastplate, then undressed and waded in. This is to record a childish incident, I know, but one excusable in a man who for days has felt tainted. This man is a stranger even to me. I do not know if the God abandoned me, or if I never touched Him at all. Even my own body is like a leper's to me. I feel shot through with disease, in my mind's endless self-concealments, in my very flesh. If I were to drain away what is sinful from myself, I would be left thinner than a leaf.

The river embalmed me in piercing coldness. It was so shallow that I stood on its bed in mid-stream, while it flowed at my neck. Oh Fausta, if we could be made pure by these waters! But purity, I see now, is an illusion.

Yet I think that at this moment I believed I would emerge from the river fit to receive the God. I felt the water's chill cut into my body as if something was being scraped off my bones and washed away. My eyes closed. I walked on the soft stream bed in a daze, fragile as a skeleton. A breeze sprang up, rustling the willows on the banks. I whispered to the God, whoever He was: "I am made new."

But little by little, even before I left the river, this feeling of renewal waned. For one thing – how irrelevant it sounds! – I felt an old sword-wound in my thigh which began to ache unbearably in the cold water. I was shivering like a coward. And soon my mind, despite itself, was filling up with the routine of tomorrow: a meeting of commanders, a new depot for provisions, an early bridgehead on the Nera river. By the time I was scrambling up the bank I had again become 'myself'.

[*In the hand of Synesius.*]

13 October

A long day's march. At mid-morning, as we were passing some potteries, a man ran at me from behind a hut. My guard, thinking he was an assassin, immediately cut him down. It turned out that he was unarmed, but diseased. Doubtless he had hoped to reach me, in the common belief that the Emperor's touch would cure him.

I no longer ask my priests what these things signify. Such incidents merely present them with a test in dissimulation, and I can see the favourable interpretation evolve behind their shifting eyes. I've come to despise them. But the omens trouble me.

Towards noon I began to feel weak. My chest was clammy inside its armour, yet when I put up my hands, my face felt cold. I stopped at a deserted farm-house near the road, and slept for an hour in the atrium, with my guard posted at the gates. I am convinced that these attacks do not come from within my body. They are directed at me from outside.

I woke up tired, but steadier. A noise inside the farther rooms had startled me, and the next moment a figure shuffled in from the peristyle courtyard. My guard had combed the place and reported nobody there, but this man had evidently been sleeping somewhere, and was rubbing the back of his neck and grumbling to himself. When he saw me he stopped dead and gazed. He was thick-set but elderly, and had a frank, rather stupid expression. He said: "What in the name of Jupiter are you doing?" I think he was the farm steward; the slaves had fled.

I said: "I'm with the army from Gaul. Weren't you warned of us?"

He stared at me in mixed suspicion and bewilderment. "Are

you carrying messages or something?" He rubbed his knuckles into his eyes. "What's that noise?"

I said, amused: "That's the army."

His hearing must have been very poor. The clash of men and wheels outside was appalling. It also occurred to me that I must have lapsed into my old habit of shouting, because he understood what I said. "Army from Gaul!" he grumbled. "What's the emperor doing in Rome then? Masturbating?"

I said I did not know.

The steward frowned at me. "Are you ill?" But he went on at once, shaking his head: "Your emperor comes right into the mountains and the one in Rome only sends his generals against him. What sort of a leader is that? A man should be better than his servants." I agree.

[*Constantine continues in his own hand.*]

Suddenly I wanted to ask questions of this old man: I saw the chance of honest, even rude replies. I had glimpsed my face in the mirror over the bed. I now wanted to inquire if this face appeared evil to him, or good. For years men have spoken to me about the radiance of the imperial countenance. And I've thought my face open and firm. Could it be that even in this I am deceived? I can trace my features in the mirror with my finger, but I am no longer sure if these do not form something ugly.

I asked him: "What do people say about this other emperor?"

But now the old man's eyes were bulging in terror, staring beneath the bed. I followed his gaze and saw my purple cloak lying on a chest beside my helmet. The next moment, with a look of extraordinary concentration and fear, he knelt in front of me, then prostrated himself, lying utterly still with his hands covering his head. "I beg Majesty's forgiveness." His voice had turned to a whimper. "I beg it. I beg . . . I thought Majesty was in Nicodemia . . . I thought . . ."

Even now he was confused. He imagined I was Diocletian, who had abdicated seven years ago. I said: "Stand up." I still thought I would ask him about my appearance.

But when he looked at me I saw the chance of truth gone from his face. Its frankness was drowned in fear. I told him to leave.

Today half western Italy appears to lie before us: wave after wave of mountains beating up against the ridge where we march. We seem very near our goal now.

After the army had stopped for the midday meal I gathered my staff on a spur and we discussed the road. Scouts report that the garrisons as far as Narni have been withdrawn; evidently the tyrant means to stare us out from behind the walls of Rome herself.

It was while we were debating this that one of my staff tribunes whispered something to Tetricus, then turned and pointed. Behind us the army showed in disconnected links of steel among the hills. The legions were resting for the noon meal on either side of the road. But to the south we looked where the hills cupped into a high valley dark with trees; down this incline, too far to be properly distinguished, something glinted and moved.

I said: "What cavalry is that?"

Tetricus frowned. Geta said: "That's not ours. None of our advance parties are so close."

"They're approaching the road three valleys back." I half ran to the crest of our ridge overlooking where our legionary cavalry was halted. So long was the view that I could see every unit of them and of the German auxiliaries. None was missing.

Tetricus said: "Those men will touch the road where the baggage and the consistory have stopped."

I thought: Fausta! Maxentius is taking Fausta.

I looked back. It was hard to tell how fast the cavalry was moving, or even to know its numbers. I felt a cold airiness in me. As I mounted my horse I wanted physically to be sick. I descended the slope at a fast trot, and began slowly to return up the road. On either side of the way the soldiers stood up and stared. I held my horse hard in, noticing the whiteness of my knuckles over the reins. The whole of my staff and guard were riding after me. Harder and harder I held the horse in against my terrible desire to gallop – to gallop like a lovesick calf in front of my entire army, back to the woman I'd repudiated. Once I drew my sword to lay the flat of it against the stallion's flanks. But instead I went on at this obscene trot, my horse's hooves sounding decorous, almost incidental.

I passed between the first ranks of the Primigenia. They cheered and waved their javelins. When I looked up at that trickle of steel in the hills it seemed hopelessly far. The gentleness of my horse's movements was unbearable. Yet I went on trotting unhurried, in command, while my heart drummed inside my cuirass.

Ahead of me the legions had now cleared the road. It lay in a long, empty avenue between their glittering ranks. We entered the lee of the hills, and the enemy cavalry vanished. The Primigenia fell behind, and we were among the Ulpia Victrix. My face had set like stone; I could feel it numb. I was jogging as stiff as a statue, except that I nodded left and right, as if reviewing the cohorts.

I do not know for how long this went on, but at last, sensing a suppressed urgency, my stallion gathered himself into a canter. My fear came fanning up into my chest and throat, and I gave him his head. The hammer of his own hooves over the polished stone panicked him, and suddenly we were galloping full stretch over the treacherously-joined slabs.

I reflect in astonishment that I went with all the carelessness of despair. The infernal clatter of the horse's feet and the amazed rivers of soldiers' faces on either side were scarcely real to me. I was clouded in my own thoughts, just as if I was lying in my bed. Over and over I accused myself for not foreseeing this. Now that it was happening it seemed obvious, even inevitable. Yet I'd been blind to it.

Maxentius was taking Fausta back.

I could drive my horse no harder. I sat helpless on him, feeling light as a plume. The waiting was unbearable. Tetricus later said that the soldiers cheered us all the way, but I never heard. I was aware only of the pounding and gasping of my great horse.

Even as I went I was touched by wonder that Maxentius should be piercing me so surely where I was most vulnerable. I do not understand this anguish at losing a woman I no longer love. Nor do I understand why I should so value her support, when she herself would half deny it. Perhaps even misery can become indispensable to a man.

The road opened on a small valley, then closed again. We panted uphill, reached a ridge, plunged to a second valley. I could see no more sign of the cavalry. They must be nearing the road now, still far ahead of us. The last standards of the Ulpia Victrix fell behind and I was amongst the first cohorts of the Minervia. Tetricus' grey stallion had dropped back, and my standard-bearer was out of sight. My own horse – a beautiful Cappadocian – was tiring. His shoulders laboured and sweated. We entered the defile before the third valley. The cold blasts of misery were beating up harder and harder inside me. All the time I had been riding I had envisaged her wrenched screaming from the carriage. But now, suddenly, I thought: Why? Why did I imagine her struggling? She herself had said that she was closer to Maxentius than to me. Wouldn't she leave with relief? And what soldier of mine would ever dare to tell me the truth of how she'd gone? How would I ever be sure?

That, I think, was what so filled me with fear as I broke into the sunlight of the third valley. The last cohorts of the Minervia were gone. I stared up at the slopes to the south. Nothing showed among their trees. The road was choked with baggage and siege engines. I charged onto the verge where groups of servants were grazing oxen and mules. The camp was strung out in the centre of the road. It looked oddly quiet. Groups of clerks and officials stared or ran from the sound of my hooves. The helmets of engineers showed between the battering-rams. They were repairing wheels. Other men were lounging among wagons or lay asleep. I thought: Maxentius must have taken her by magic, it's so hushed.

Then I saw the canopied top of her carriage. It had been stopped on the north side of the road. I plunged across between unhitched carts. I don't know what I expected to see. There was nobody there. The carriage windows were closed. A small summer tent had been pitched nearby. Her bodyguard were grazing their mounts a short distance away.

I threw myself from my horse as her guards ran towards me. My limbs were trembling. I pulled at one of the carriage doors. There was nothing inside but a few blankets and Fausta's cloak. I turned and scanned the hillsides. They showed nothing. I ran to the tent. I heard armour crashing on the road as the first of my guard arrived. I burst in through the flap, breaking its cords.

Inside, beyond two folding chairs and a chest, with her back against the tent, Fausta stood rigid. Her companion was clutching a heavy lamp, which she dropped the moment I entered. They stared at me, astonished. Fausta said: "What's happened?"

I turned and glared from the entrance, as if we might be surrounded. But the first of my own men were thronging about it, covered in dust, their swords drawn. I went back inside, dropping the tent flap behind me. "Has nobody been here?"

"Nobody," Fausta said. "Oh Gaius, what's the matter?" She came, softly laid her hand on my forearm, and eased the sword from my fingers. She was staring into my face with puzzled anxiety. I could tell that she was afraid for my sanity.

I said: "We saw cavalry moving down the valley opposite. But they must have been our own. I don't understand it."

"What did you think they were doing?"

I found myself holding her shoulders to make sure that she was there. Strange how at such moments the sense of touch is so important. I said: "I thought they were going to take you away."

My expression must have showed how weak I was. We stared at one another. For a second her face was touched by the softness which I had not thought I'd see again. The palms of her hands came to rest lightly on my breastplate. The next moment her blush had disappeared as if I had imagined it, and she said: "You do look peculiar, Gaius." She dabbed at my forehead with her sleeve. "You've got white eyebrows."

I felt a fool, standing between those two women, glaring about me. I noticed they'd merely been playing backgammon. I heard Tetricus outside the tent, asking for admission. He bowed to Fausta, cradling his helmet; his head was steaming like a horse. He grinned at me. "They were our own men, Augustus. Scouts. Their centurion had been taken ill, the dolt. They were bringing him to camp." He made as if to go, then turned and grimaced. "We lost a man and two horses back on the road. One of your orderlies smashed his skull like an egg."

After he had gone Fausta said: "I'm not worth that man, Gaius."

"I'll judge that." I did not know what to say to her. There seemed nothing more to say. But I wanted to remain with her until I was sure that she was there. I was feeling naked, as if I had left bits of myself scattered down the road. I caught myself staring at my own wife.

XXI

Fausta to Marina at Nice.

Carsulae, 16 October

YOUR servant arrived this morning, Marina, but guess what had happened to your letter? Soaked! Your man had been robbed on the road near Genoa, and forced to sell his waterproof cloak. So now I have the strangest document. Half the words are washed away, while the other half tantalises. 'Lucul . . . ining . . . cent . . .' What can that be? Is Lucullus dining with centaurs? How impressive. It's the best letter you've written me.

But time presses and I must send your man back with word of my own. The trouble with my news is that I no longer know what is significant. And some of it makes me afraid.

Last night, Mari, I dreamt that Gaius was standing above my bed. I knew that he had been stabbed, although I could not see the dagger, and the blood of his wound was splashing on to my face. He asked me to draw out the blade and ease his pain, but I could not move. I seemed to be weighted down by iron.

Can this mean that he is going to be killed, Mari? I cannot believe it. I don't. The dream was so cruel that I long for an interpretation, but I dare not mention it to anybody. Perhaps it only obsesses me because of my incarceration, day after day, in this closed carriage. Even small things start to loom large here. So I will try to put it out of my mind.

All day we move exposed along the crests of ridges, so that I expect at any time to look beyond the hills and glimpse the western sea. My uselessness starts to madden me. Livilla and I do nothing but play backgammon. The siege of Rome becomes less important than whether I throw a six or a twelve. Then I hate myself for the pettiness and boredom of it, and turn morose. She and I argue like teenage girls. Her tastes and affectations gnaw at me, even when she is not indulging them. Her only reasons for wanting to reach Rome are to visit scent shops and flirt in the Gardens of Sallust. At one time our servants brought us food from the camp kitchens, and we ate inside the carriage. But the smell of fish sauce put us both in such a temper that we now pitch our summer tent at midday, and eat in that.

As for the nights, they have turned cold, and our beds are often made up in the carriage. Livilla says I talk in my dreams.

You will have realised by now that I am happier. Why this should be I cannot define. But two days ago something strange occurred. The army had halted for the noon meal and our tent was set up by the roadside in a quiet valley full of trees. The thick upland pasture had turned even the oxen silent, and most of the servants had fallen asleep. Livilla and I sat in our tent playing the ridiculous backgammon and waiting for lunch – heroic women! I remember thinking that within ten days we would be at the gates of Rome.

Then we heard something crash across the road. There was a sound of hooves and scattering stones. We sat frozen. My guards were shouting and running.

We got to our feet. I imagined that Maxi had sent men to capture me. I had an idea that he wanted to punish me – because I am a traitor in his eyes, just as I am in those of Gaius. In these seconds of panic I realised with faint surprise that I would kill myself if I was taken back to him. I thought: I must, after all, be closer to Gaius – or wish to be. To return to Maxi would be a kind of death. Even while the sound of hooves came close I envisaged the mockery in his eyes, as if he said: 'You've been pretending to be an empress, but I know you.' He does know me too, and his knowledge belittles me. Yet – how strange, Marina! – he would not understand what 'belittles' means, whereas I now do.

We heard our carriage doors being wrenched open, then feet trampling near the tent.

Livilla is an unpredictable woman. You'd expect her to be useless under such strain. She's recently taken to cradling a ball of fragrant amber as if the odour of honest soldiers hurt her not-so-patrician nostrils; and ever since Verona she's been scared of every horse that whinnied. But I confess that now, while I stood transfixed, she rushed to tie up the thongs of the entrance, then seized a lamp with the look of a maenad. The next moment the flap was ripped open and Gaius was standing there. Oh Marina, he looked as if he'd been in a carnival! His helmet was gone and his hair was pale with dust. His face too was covered in it, so that his eyes glared out most strangely. I would have laughed if I had not been so afraid. But the working of his jaw made him appear mad. I had the idea that he thought I was with another man. His face wore that ferocious, trembling aspect – I've seen it before when some official has been too attentive to me; but now it was uncontrolled.

He shouted: "Has anybody been here?"

I tried to calm him. Apparently he'd mistaken a body of scouts for the enemy, and had galloped four miles down the road to us. When he embraced me his expression was most pathetic, almost lost. I did not know what to say.

Later

A messenger has just arrived asking that I join Gaius this evening. It will be the first time since Faventia. I feel like a girl. I'm even shaking. But this, I know, is a perversity. What have I to do with love? Perhaps, instead, we'll create something new out of our honesty. I always said I wanted friendship. So perhaps we will create friendship. 'Better a hovel on rock, than a palace on water.' Who said that? My mind is a lumber yard of half-remembered things!

I must end this. As usual, my vanity will take an hour to choose my dress and jewellery.

I sometimes wonder if I will tell my child about love. No, I think I'll confine his hopes to sexual friendship. Then if he discovers this other thing it will be free from rumour, something unforeseen which he can assess for himself. It may be then that he will not find it at all.

Good-bye, gentle cousin. My next letter will come from – where? Rome, perhaps, or else it will not come.

Here, by the by, is a strange thing. I believe I could have loved a plain, small man. Explain that.

XXII

Journal-Memoir of Constantine.

Carsulae, 16 October

CARSULAE surrenders at our approach: a walled town with triumphal arch to Trajan. It is good for the men's morale to see these prefects grovelling in the gateways of their defensible cities. If every fortress had been defended between here and the Alps, we would still be besieging Turin.

As we were marching through the forum I looked up and saw my father's statue gazing down on me from a place of honour. Why it had been preserved here, when our images had been thrown down in every province of the southern Empire, I do not know. But I was very moved. I summoned the elders of the city, expressed my gratitude and exempted them from taxes for the year to come. Afterwards, when the streets had been cleared by curfew, I stood beneath that strong, beloved face, and poured out a libation to his memory.

At dusk I set up headquarters in a disused temple to Diana, then did what I have long meant to do: I sent a message to Fausta to join me after supper. Sitting in the sanctuary, lit by torches along the walls, I waited in preoccupation while members of the consistory came to see me on business. They all looked anxious and nervy. This mood seems to be spreading through the imperial staff. The temple itself, in its fetid darkness, filled me with gloom. Only Bishop Hosius greeted me with smiles and assurances. He wore the silver cross on his chest. It hung there in the torchlight like the talisman of our hope.

The moment Fausta arrived I dismissed my officials and we were left alone. We sat in high-backed chairs, opposite one another, rather formally. She looked restrained but attentive, dressed very simply in white. I too felt composed, almost grave.

I have discovered that if I examine the face of a friend for long, he becomes foreign to me. This now happened with Fausta. I was trying so intently to reappraise her, that her face lost its familiarity altogether. I watched it as if it were a stranger's. Its flat eyebrows, I thought, gave it a slightly cruel look, which was deceptive. Fausta is not cruel, except perhaps to herself. The darkness and glitter of her eyes did not quite dispel this impression. She is, I suppose, handsome rather than pretty. Her hair is coarse and her complexion poor, but its pallor beautiful. The face struck me as frank, intense, yet rather cold.

I said: "Tomorrow I will double your bodyguard."

"That's not necessary, Gaius. You need men for more important things." She settled her cloak over the chair behind her shoulders, then said: "I'm not running away." She pushed this remark cautiously towards me, like an offering.

I remembered the panic of that four-mile ride over flagstones; even now it was lodged, very small and cold, under my ribs. "Your brother may still try to abduct you."

"I don't know what he'd want with me."

"Aren't we fighting over you?" I was joking, pretending to joke. "Sometimes I feel we are."

"A poor Helen of Troy!" she laughed.

Her laughter warmed us. For a while we talked about apparently trivial things, but all the time I had a feeling that we cautiously approached one another. I was reminded of the Pyrrhic advance of the legions – two steps, then a pause, two steps. . . . It was as if we were expecting to alight on something corrupted or hurtful. And perhaps if we had been trying to re-establish what we were, we would have foundered. But we were wiser than that.

After a while I started speaking about the Sun, and was pulled up short by her saying: "I'm sorry. I seem blind to these things."

I remembered how such turmoils irritated her. But I didn't rail at her. I avoided talking about them. This gave me a peculiar feeling. I've never learnt to avoid. I said: "Do you remember the Christian persecutions?"

"I was in Milan during those. Were there any there? I don't recall." She frowned. "But I remember looking down from the palace window in Aquileia and seeing men being led out of the prefecture to prison. My maid said not to let them glimpse me in case they made the sign of the cross."

"They say their cross is magic."

"Yes," she said, "yes, it may be so." But I know she does not care for the Christians. "That's how the persecution began. Christians on the staff of Diocletian made the sign of the cross. Or was that just one of my father's stories?"

"Did he say that?"

"Yes, but he used to lie like a Syrian."

We laughed together. I cushioned my shoulders back into the chair. The smoke of the torches was coiling thick about the ceiling; their flames illumined rivers of damp down the walls. Above us a decaying fresco showed the virgin goddess Diana pursuing Actaeon – he who by chance had seen her naked as she

144

bathed. The vengeful figure of the huntress, with a pair of shaggy hounds, showed beyond Fausta's head in the dim light.

I said: "The bishop says there's no selflessness in love between men and women." We were sitting looking straight at one another. We both realised what we were doing, feeling which ground was firm and which unsafe.

"I never expected selflessness." Fausta spoke quietly, as if in deference to the temple. "It's more practical to hope for comfort, I think."

"Comfort." I'm less disdainful of this word than I used to be. I said: "You were always clearer-headed than me." I found this quite easy to say. Yet it was a veiled apology for my old fury at her incapacity to love. Apology is another thing of which I have grown incapable, and this was all the sorrow I have ever expressed to her for my four years' harshness.

But she must have understood, because she said very deliberately, as if it were a manifesto: "I think I'm capable of respect and perhaps of affection."

I smiled at her. It struck me that she looked much older, lined. Perhaps it was the play of flames over her face. Affection seemed an odd possibility. The only person who feels that for me is Cecrops. I said to reassure her: "I don't want to talk about love."

My words sounded lonely in the silence. Fausta was staring at her hands. I watched them too: white on the white dress. I think I am obsessed by appearances. I wish I had a portrait of Fausta as she was. Did I imagine the bloom on her skin? But the only picture of her I know is the mural of a child in the palace at Aquileia: a wide-eyed nothing.

I said: "I envy passionless affection." I think I said this to please her.

She answered to my surprise: "There's no point in accusing yourself."

This anxiety not to hurt one another is new. And so is this tempered respect. Why we should still respect one another at all, I don't know. We've done all we can to destroy that.

Fausta suddenly said: "Gaius — " then stopped. I waited. She licked her lips uncertainly, and went on: "I dreamt last night that you were wounded. Your blood was falling on my face. What does that mean?"

"I don't know."

"You asked me to pull out the dagger to ease you. But I couldn't move."

I stared away from her. The guttering torches were sending violent ribbons of light up and down the walls. "I don't know." I suddenly did not want to think about it.

She got up and stood near, but did not like to touch me. I held out my hand to her. She put hers in it, a little as if she was giving me a utensil. I said: "Do you want to go back to your quarters now?"

"If you wish me to."

I could not tell what she wanted. I think she was indifferent. "I'd rather you stayed," I said. "But not if it disgusts you."

"I was never disgusted by love," she answered. "I was frightened by it."

I said: "There's nothing to frighten you now."

We walked to the antechamber where my servants had set up my bed. It looked narrow and comfortless, covered with coarse rugs. We undressed by the faltering light of the torches through the open door. She bent to pick up her dress. When she straightened in front of me I saw her breasts, intricate and beautiful in the soft light. But they were a little remote to me now, as if I looked at them through muslin. She stood close against me. I felt her hands trickling down my back until they held my buttocks, and she laughed. I kissed her mouth to stop this nervous laughter, and lowered her to the bed.

We lay together gravely, almost like a ceremony. She moved my hands about her body, warming herself. I think she was happier for my silence. Momentarily my desire wakened a cry in me which I did not utter. Strange how there arises out of lust this fleeting worship. Her self-possession did not irritate me. It seemed perfectly natural. I took her quietly, and after a while we fell asleep.

The trumpet of the fourth watch woke me. A soldier hears these signals in his sleep and knows the time the moment he wakes. My eyes felt sore. The air was smoky with dying torches. Their light covered the room in a pink sheen. Fausta's face lay close to mine, as it often has; but it seemed enclosed and sour now, although its lips were upturned in the smile which used to attract me. I looked away from her. Through the doorway, in the fitful light, a frescoed Actaeon was being torn eternally by the hounds of Diana. Fausta murmured something in her sleep. I stared at her as if this murmur might signify something. She was silent again. I looked back through the door, closed my eyes. I tried to think of what I had to do today: men, food, horses. But inside me something ached and cried out. I felt an emptiness more total than the gap of our separation had been. I know that there is no real love, that this is the dream of children. Yet as I clenched my eyes shut I gazed away from Fausta in my mind, imagining that there was something beyond her.

I find I do this still. I cannot help it.

XXIII

Bishop Hosius, to the Consecrated Virgin
Emilia, his sister, at Cordoba.

17 October

My dear, I sense some sadness in your letter, even obstinacy as to what I say about the love between men and women. If our dear Crispus had lived, I know you would have made a most grave and modest wife. But you, my sister, are married to a nobler Bridegroom.

The curses of the flesh do not only plague the humble, Emilia. On today's march the great Augustus himself sought me out as he was passing the consistory, and for half an hour we rode side by side and alone in the centre of the army. I see a great change in him. Something painful has come between himself and his wife. All the time we spoke he held his stomach with one hand, as if it ached, and the veins stood out from his forehead like scars. God has indeed cast him down. He speaks of solitude and the farness of divinity. And love he does not believe in at all. I told him that 'God is love, and he who dwells in love dwells in God.' But he only looked at me with his fierce, puzzled frown and said: "The God is far away."

I sense he believes that all people, himself especially, have been abandoned to chaos. It is this heresy which I cannot endure. I said: "Eternity, forgive me (for one must speak to him like this). Men are of God. Dreadfully tainted, Augustus, but of God. We can be pure through faith." Then I held up the cross to him, as I did once before, looking down on clouds near Mevania.

He said nothing, but he did not seem angry. He stared at it with a look which I cannot describe to you – uncertain and brooding. I even thought he might take it from my hands. He thinks all the time. His brain must be a terrible fire. This man, my sister, will become either a devil or a saint.

At last he said, but as if ashamed of himself: "Point it at Rome."

So I held the cross towards Rome. The Augustus believes, as I do, that the tyrant is sending demons against us, and he has no god to shield him. My Emilia, this great man is like a baby. He understands nothing. He trusts nobody. He cannot pray. And it was strange to ride with him along that great descending spur of the Apennines, pointing the symbol of our Christ at the city of corruption. For Rome, say all reports, has grown huge and empty like a rotten pumpkin. Her people are vicious, her senators fickle and her institutions moribund. The whole city is a living lie.

"You will pluck this city, Eternity!" I said.

He demanded: "What is that to you? Maxentius has never persecuted Christians."

Then I told him that tyranny against any man is an affront to our God and that there is no person, no insect, no rock, which God does not hear. This was hard for the Augustus to understand. Pagans believe that deities bandy men about, indulge or forget them, even intermarry with them. Our God must seem strangely constant to such men. God will not endure the suffering of the innocent, and because of this I told the Augustus what I believe: that Christ is marching with our army.

The Augustus listened to me with deep attention, saying very little. And now I dared to remind him of how God had avenged the persecution of His worshippers. Once such words would have imperilled my very life, but not any more. And I am fortunate that those emperors who have shed the blood of the saints have also been the enemies of the Augustus. While I spoke I watched his profile for any change of mood. His eyes were shadowed by his helmet, but I could see his hard jaws and mouth. All the time I recounted the deaths of the persecutors, he never spoke.

And what an awesome roll, my sister, they are! Nero, who crucified St. Peter and beheaded St. Paul, and will appear at the Last Judgement as the forerunner of the Devil – he stabbed himself in the throat in ignominy, and died among slaves. Next, Domitian, murdered as soon as he began to persecute. No trace of this once great emperor is left. His statues were thrown down, his every inscription erased, and all his acts repealed. As for the torturer Decius who came after him, he was slain with his children by the barbarians, and his body thrown to the birds.

And what father does not frighten his naughty children by recounting the fate of the Emperor Valerian, who was taken prisoner by the Persians and became the footstool of the Great King? Every time Sapor mounted his horse or chariot he trod on the back of the persecutor, until at last he had him flayed alive and hung his skin up in the temples of the Persian gods. I myself met a man who'd seen it – a Greek who had served at the court in Ctesiphon. He mistook it for a blackened banner.

Nor is this all, my sister. Within our own memory the Emperor Aurelian was murdered by his trusted generals even before his edict against the faithful had reached the confines of the Empire. The monster Severus was defeated and executed not six years ago. And the arch-persecutor Maximian committed suicide after his defeat by Constantine himself.

Lastly I remembered Galerius, whom the Augustus, of course, hated most. To him the Lord sent a wasting disease which rotted his bowels and bred worms in his genitals. His servants called on Apollo and Aesculapius, but his guts putrefied until the stench of him pervaded the palace and even, some say, the whole city. With just such a malady did God kill Herod, who murdered the Holy Innocents. And now Galerius published an edict of repentance, and died.

The moment I'd finished speaking, the Augustus turned his horse without a word and rode away to his staff.

[The letter closes with some observations on a uniform penitential code for the Spanish churches.]

XXIV

Commonplace Book of Synesius.

BETWEEN Mevania and Carsulae the land and the villages were empty. This gave the more cowardly members of the consistory (myself and my mule) the ridiculous feeling that we were being watched, whereas obviously the fewer people about, the less likely this is. The impressionability of civilians in the field is worse than that of soldiers in the cities.

Carsulae surrendered without a murmur, and the Augustus exempted its prefecture from a year's taxes because he found a statue of his father still standing in the forum. Nobody noticed that the plinth of the statue had been broken and cunningly joined again. Its left flank was discoloured where it had been lying in drainage, I imagine. Several of the city councillors saw me examining it, and blushed scarlet. But I had no heart to tell the Augustus.

Our road now descends all the time. Yesterday we approached the great chasm of the Nera river, and saw the viaduct which Augustus Caesar built of marble nearly three centuries ago. It stood perfect, spanning the abyss on four arches a hundred feet in the air, and carried us across suspended between earth and sky. Some of the Gallic legionaries were afraid of it, and refused to cross until they had thrown charms into the ravine. The ratio of brains to muscle in this army, I calculate, is that of certain spiders: a miniscule head on a host of hairy legs. If we could be envisaged symbolically, that is how we would look – a monstrous spider shambling along to Rome. I try to enjoy this conceit, while my mule tortures me.

Beyond the ravine the wealthy town of Narni opened its gates to us. Its garrison had fled. It stands high on a spur above the river, very powerful, and the Augustus has manned it strongly – to cover our retreat if we are defeated, I suspect. He now bullies his staff without mercy. We all go in fear of him. He seems scarcely to sleep, and spends the early night visiting the legions. Yet he is up before dawn. Jagged lines have appeared around his mouth, and his cheeks are scooped out like craters. He must have a body of iron.

All the rumours are now that Maxentius will take the field against us. The numbers of his Praetorian Guard alone must almost equal those of our army. This, I imagine, is why Constantine today left the Empress behind at Narni, with some of his civil staff and many siege engines.

I dined with them last night in the villa where they slept. The Augustus chooses his quarters for convenience, not comfort, but yesterday he had alighted on a luxurious little house, with sheets laid over its skylights to preserve the heat. We ate on couches inlaid with ivory and tortoiseshell, and since Tetricus, Geta and the Marshal joined us we must have resembled so many street dogs squatting on palace furniture. But during campaign the Augustus eats no better than his men. We were served the plainest fare, even salted pork, and the wine was that sour brew which is inflicted on soldiers in the field by some quirk of the quartermaster. We needed only pease-pudding to complete my misery.

I was placed near Constantine. He and the Empress, on their last evening together, reclined side by side, and seemed to look out at the rest of us with a troubled reserve. I was reminded of the unsmiling effigies which recline on family sarcophagi, challenging the outsider to penetrate the secret of their dead. He and she are no longer intense together, but conciliatory, even delicate. They continue to look each other in the eyes when they are speaking: a hopeful sign. She has fallen into the habit of lightly plucking his sleeve before she addresses him. And I noticed that one of his personal rings – a mounted diamond – was on her middle finger. She examined this several times during the meal. In earlier days the Augustus used to rest his chin on her shoulder; he no longer does that.

Tetricus was eating beside me. I've never shared the consistory's view that he is merely a bluff soldier. Unvarnished he certainly is, but then most of those surrounding the Augustus are varnished into imbecile reflections of one another. I now heard him say: "The diamond symbolises constancy." I turned to see his gnarled face smiling – his teeth, unfortunately, are mostly broken – and looking in the same direction as I had been. "Things are better over there," he said. "Less, but better."

Tetricus is sparing of any words, let alone gossip. I greedily

seized my chance. "You think His Eternity's mind is clear?"
I whispered. "Will it be clear on the battlefield?"

"Don't worry, Secretary." The prefect nodded. "I think his
mind saves its clarity for the battlefield."

We had outlandish entertainment that night. One of the city
decurions had sent his *stupidus* to us: a dwarf with a deformed
face. All the wretch's bones seemed to retract evenly above the
jaw, giving him the look of a donkey, and his ears, by chance or
artifice, had been elongated almost to the crown of his skull.
This obscene creature gambolled ceaselessly in front of our
couches, his huge head flopping out of control. The thought of
him pervades the whole evening, so that I find it hard to remember anybody else. But on the couch opposite me, I think, was
Geta, forgettable and unforgetting – I believe I dislike this dapper
little man because we are too similar.

I also recall the Marshal, generally so undemonstrative, growing drunk on soured wine. He was clearly going to flirt with
anybody close to him. On one side was Tetricus, a forbidding
prospect. On the other lay the Lady Politta, who was battling
with her salted pork. She proved amenable. No one appreciates a
soldier as a woman does – and *vice versa*. The Marshal finally
dropped asleep across her thighs, a much-trodden avenue I
suspect. And all the time the eerie dwarf was dancing and
balancing things on his head.

The Augustus and the Empress talked together in the solemn,
matter-of-fact way which is new to them. I've noticed before
how lamp-light darkens those lustrous eyes of hers. I saw his hand
rest for a second on her forearm. She was saying: "I won't have
you leave a single soldier here on my account. It's ignominious,
Gaius. It turns me into a burden. I don't care if you leave me
here alone."

He answered: "I'm detailing six hundred men. It's nothing to
do with you. That's the minimal garrison for this place."

I noticed his gaze drop from hers. I rather think a garrison of
three hundred could hold Narni. I suspect she thought the same.
But we are not soldiers, and this may be my or her illusion. The
Augustus pursed his lips and said nothing more.

I don't recall much about the rest of the evening, except for an
increasing idea that the mean eyes of the dwarf, as he lolled and
capered, were regarding us all with veiled contempt. But this

was better than dining with the secretariats. These military men are only a few days from battle, yet they eat their revolting food heartily and mostly seem to evade thought. The secretariats, on the other hand, do nothing but think. A breathless foreboding pervades every meal. The Masters of Letters whisper together and roll their eyes, and if somebody drops a knife or spoon its clatter splits the tent.

Towards the evening's end I heard Constantine say to the Empress: "I'll send you word of anything significant. On no account must you leave Narni." Then he looked at her in a way which in him I would call gentle, and added: "If there's a siege you must go to the villa which your cousin promised you, at Otricolum. The weather will be milder there."

I waited for her reply. I kept my eyes on my meal. I heard her say distinctly: "I would rather be with you."

I imagined that they were staring at one another, after their exacting fashion. It seemed to me that they were not at all interested in the villa, but that each was saying: 'I give you this. I do not love you, but I give you this.'

Early this morning, as we prepared to march, I watched the Augustus emerge from headquarters with the Empress and his close staff. He advanced the imperial standard, ordered his commanders to precede him on the road, and summoned his horse. Then we saw an extraordinary thing. The Empress started to weep. She tried to conceal this with her hand, but could not. In a woman whose husband may be going to his death a few tears might be thought a decent duty. But in the Empress Fausta they were utterly unexpected. I think even the Augustus was taken aback. He took her hand formally, and kissed her farewell while the tears rolled down her cheeks. Nobody made a sound. For a moment they stood against one another with their heads bowed, as if lamenting something. Then he mounted his horse and we moved away.

XXV

Geta, Master of the Offices, to Constantine.

20 October

FINAL report and estimate of enemy numbers and regiments. Full particulars attached, collating to a total of 92,000 men.

Also attached: a full estimate of our own forces, including advance detachments: a total of 40,400 men.

Reports are unanimous that Rome is not preparing for a siege, and that the tyrant will take the field.

May the Augustus live for ever.

XXVI

Constantine to Fausta at Narni.

48th Mile-Post, Via Flaminia, 20 October

M Y Empress: you are stronger than your tears, or I would not write this to you.

If we are defeated, I may not return. Should this be so, Tetricus has orders to withdraw the army beyond Narni back to Gaul. You are to go with him. Geta assumes command if Tetricus is killed.

Would you regret our marriage? I could not blame you. For four years I accused you in the name of my own brutishness, which I called love. A pretty device. You were wise not to let me trample you. I esteem you more and more.

XXVII

Fausta to Constantine.

Narni, 21 October

Y ES, Gaius, if you do not come back I will withdraw with the army, provided it exists, to Gaul. And we will avenge you. Should my brother capture me (and you may be sure he'll try) I imagine I will kill myself – not because I'm cowardly, but because I am tired. I don't want to return to who I was, or realise what I am.

I write this under the strain of our farewell, because there is no other way that I will dare to express a truth to you. It's this: if you should die, my life too will be over. This fact makes me angry. It betrays my emptiness and turns me into a slave. But in part, too, it is a tribute to you, my husband. You are more absolute than other men. This makes me petulant with you, and afraid. *But I cannot do with less.*

I will send you this confession before I change my mind and the other Fausta tears it up. Foolish to write what you no longer wish to hear.

You say I was wise not to let myself be trampled — but how bitterly I wish that I was soft enough to fall underfoot! It is not wisdom, Gaius, it is fear and coldness which preserve me. They will preserve me always — and from everything. Yes, from life itself. And from love above all. I am not afraid to use that word — I don't despise it, as you do. Yes, I wish I had loved you. How I wish it! And I wish that you could still say 'love' and believe. Oh Gaius, what have I done to you?

[This letter was never sent. It was found among the Empress' private papers after her execution by Constantine in 326.]

XXVIII

Journal-Memoir of Constantine.

38th Mile-Post, Via Flaminia, 22 October

WE approach the last palisade of the Apennines — a silhouette heavy with storm. Scouts have made contact with the enemy cavalry, which now hangs about unseen in valleys on our flanks. I strengthen the forward detachments. We march through a land utterly desolate. The villages are deserted. Their abandoned dogs howl in the fields. The weather is warm, oppressive even, but I can see my own breath and my hands feel stiff on the reins. In the hills the autumn trees afford thin cover for an attack. It seems like winter already. The earth is dying. Everything round us is emptied of the God's life. Yet to the west the storm looks heavy, and the air is thick with foreboding.

At noon a rainbow appeared in the sky in front of us. Sacrovir tells me that this is the goddess Iris coming down to earth to effect a change in the affairs of men. But what change?

A few minutes afterwards, while we were riding through a

copse without any sign of a wind, a pine tree crashed across the road not ten paces in front of me, barring my path. My whole retinue was aghast. No omen could be worse. I shouted so that they could all hear: "Even the trees of Rome fall at our feet!" and the moment passed. But my heart sank. The air is sick with evil.

All day the storm has been piled in front of us like a solid wall. We are moving into the jaws of demons, I am certain of this now. The tyrant's power is nearly tangible, and it's said that he has sacrificed so often to the goddess Hecate that her statue smiles at him. Even on the march the army is quiet and tense. The soldiers mutter together. We move with a nervous clanking. My horse's hooves patter on the stone. Sometimes I have the idea that this paved road is a causeway over a bottomless lake. At least twice I have had to steel myself before riding my horse on to the verge. Even the land behind us seems no longer familiar, although we have conquered it. It has returned to hostility.

I think of Fausta. Although we are only eighteen miles beyond Narni, she seems far away. Last night my whole body groaned with the loss of her, and my thoughts strayed to other women, as if I might achieve with them the innocence which she and I could not. This was puerile. In the next few years, should I live, I shall beget children for the continuance of the Empire. But when this is done I shall vow my chastity to Cybele, or in one of the temples of the Christian god.

On today's march I found myself dwelling on those emperors who persecuted the Christians, and on what became of them. It is hard, of course, to know why these men met their end. But the list of them is awesome, and tells that this god, if god he is, must be more powerful than we suppose. I myself recall that when I was still a young man in Nicodemia some great spirit struck at the palace of the Emperor Diocletian there. It cannot have been long after he promulgated his first edict against the Christians. I was practising swordplay with friends in one of the courtyards, when a heavy storm broke. We had no sooner reached the porticoes than a thunderclap shook us to the roots. I looked up to see a lance of light fall on the towers of the palace. I was thrown on my face. When I got up again all the private chambers of the Emperor had been reduced to a sea of rubble.

Yesterday I noticed the bishop riding with the court. The

cross shone on his chest. I wanted to inquire of him whether I myself, without knowing, can have been the agent of this god, because it was I who defeated the persecutor Maximian. But the Augustus cannot ask what other men can, and I let him pass, saluting me.

Today, towards evening, we reached the Tiber. The bridge was still standing. My retinue became excited and rode down its banks close to the water, which flowed strongly among silver-leaved trees. I know that I was expected to make sacrifice to the river, but I could not. It is the protector of Rome, a city I have grown to hate. I gave orders to pitch camp on the far side, then sat my horse and watched the first cohorts of the Primigenia as they crossed. On the bridge beneath, somebody had scrawled: 'Matricide'. But the word no longer appalled me; it even ack-knowledged my power. I have sunk to this.

Tetricus glanced up and said: "The storm will break tonight."

For three days we have not seen the sun. I've stopped looking up at the sky. The nights descend out of a deepening grey, and I dread them. Often I imagine that if the sun shone again for a long time, very strong and bold above my army, I should start once more to believe. But I think not. The night has entered my eyes.

Sometimes I feel as I felt in nightmares as a child: that darkness is a tomb. Not the peace of death, but a terrible unknown. I used to sleepwalk. Night after night I would wake up in blackness in my mother's home at Drepanum not knowing where I was, to hear my fists beating on the walls. I can still feel the stone's coldness, and the crumbling plaster under my nails. The walls reverberated like a pit. Until at last my hands would find the panelling of an alcove, or I would discover the shape of moonlight in a doorway, and then I would remember. Sometimes, too, Cecrops would come with a lamp (he already seemed so old!) and carry me back to my bed.

Today at dusk I waited until the last cohorts had crossed the Tiber. They cheered me, clashing their javelins, and the Ulpia Victrix broke into martial song. My soldier's eye tells me they look confident and strong. But they do not know what I know. As I watched them, I felt as if the road on which they marched was thin as ice, and their clash and singing died small in the silence of the hills.

Sometimes, when I see the trust in some of these men's faces, I have felt unable to look the poorest legionary in the eyes; at other times I am so angry with the God that I'm afraid I will blaspheme. Priests tell us that evil men turn wilfully from the divine, and refuse to worship it. But this is not so. No, the gods turn from men. Men desire them, but they are not there. So where are they? Where?

What a power of worship is in us!

Tonight, as I write this, the storm is breaking. The noise on our leather tents sounds like clattering hail. I do not think I shall write in this journal again. If I live, I shall refurbish it for the Sacred Historian. The people want a hero, not a man.

But the future is unimaginable. I can only feel it, like a physical presence, to be waiting out there in the rain: a great abyss. What future can there be without the God? That is why I see only this chasm: infinite, for ever.

It is unendurable. Could I find God in the rain? What God?

I, Gaius Constantine, out of the anger in my heart and the love I bear my army, write this: there is no God. I have been led astray.

My mind is splitting. I look at my words and I am afraid of the deity I deny.

Where? Where?

This sense of imminence: I feel that if I go and draw back my tent flap, the God will be there. Yet he does not exist. And Hecate closes out the light.

[Constantine's journal ends here. He was less than 40 miles from Rome.]

XXIX

Commonplace Book of Synesius.

22 October

SUNSET: we reached the Tiber and crossed over by a stout bridge. A storm lingers in the west, but does not break. It's been an uneventful day: the weather crisp above us, the sun shining. Apparently the Augustus refused to sacrifice at the river. Tetricus was the only one who dared suggest it, and Constantine cried "To what god? To what god?" and turned his back. Indeed it would be pleasant if this wasteful and boring ritual was discontinued.

The Augustus dismissed me early this evening, telling me I looked tired. This is true. As for him, he resembles a towering ghost.

23 October

Last night, with the wind blowing from the west, the enemy set fire to stubble fields. We woke to see long curtains of flame advancing towards us, although the ground was damp with early storm. We lost a few baggage animals which bolted, and the fire died at our earthworks. But it was a disturbed sleep.

The morning brought slow progress. Scouts coming and going. Rumours. The skirmishing round our flanks remained invisible, but could be distinctly heard. I rode for two hours with the imperial retinue, and saw that the Augustus was tense as a bowstring. His voice has turned hoarse, and the sweat leaks from under his helmet. His tribunes are starting to whisper.

We passed tombs on either side of the road. They line it all the way to Rome. In one, whose wall had split, the mummified corpse of a woman was sitting up and facing west. The augurs of the priesthood huddled about it like rooks before sending interpretations to the Augustus. How I detest them!

This evening, while we were still marching, I became sick and was given a place in the carriage of the camp commandant. But now I am up again, unsteady and glad to dine alone in my tent. The air is suddenly oppressive and the consistory is seething with nerves. This makes me depressed and anxious. For the first time I allow myself to contemplate the coming battle. It occurs to me how tenacious of life we become when we are old.

18th Mile-Post, Via Flaminia, 24 October

THE nightmare has happened. It will engulf us all.
I witnessed it myself, because I was riding close behind the

Augustus all morning, awaiting orders. So I became a humble part of history.

The army had cleared the last foothills and was moving out into the plain. The skirmishing had stopped. We could hear nothing. The Augustus gave some directives to Sacrovir and the flanking cavalry. I forget what they were, but his voice sounded toneless. I also remember an odd stiffness about the set of his shoulders and the way his legs gripped his horse's flanks.

To our left the peak of Mount Soracte rose in the morning light. It was crowned by a temple to Apollo of the Sun. We crossed a farmed ridge while the peak disappeared and re-appeared among trees. Several times I saw the Augustus rub his eyes and stare at the sky, which was constantly clouded. Then we came to a place where the mountain filled the whole horizon, towering black and somehow tragic. The staff was riding in total silence. Everything around us was silent. Somewhere over to our right the fortified town of Falerii sent no negotiator. Everyone was awaiting the outcome of the battle.

It must have been almost noon. I remember that the sun burst from the clouds and beat on us quite strongly, because the tribune riding by my side took off his helmet. I cannot have been more than twenty paces behind Constantine. He was riding between Tetricus and Geta, a little in front of both, with the Marshal and the imperial standard behind. Something in the way he sat his saddle – his body rising almost clear of its crest – gave a feeling of extraordinary agitation.

Then his horse stopped dead. I heard him cry out. The Marshal said that his eyes were glazed, and that he cried "Fausta? Look! God, god!" For a moment he sat upright, rigid, then he buckled against the horse's neck, and quite slowly, with the reins still in his hands, slid over its shoulder.

Somehow he landed on his feet. But for a full minute he remained with his face buried against the horse, clasping the sides of his head. I saw that his neck glistened in a sheen of sweat and his hands trembled. Tetricus and Geta had both dismounted and some orderlies made frightened gestures at supporting him. One of the miseries of an emperor is that nobody has the courage to touch him in trouble. He is meant to be above it. Only the old servant Cecrops, who bears his armour, dared to stump forward with a skinful of water, and threw it in the Augustus' face. For a few seconds Constantine glared about him, clutching at his breastplate, then he shook his head violently and mounted his horse unaided.

We were all aware that something momentous had happened. During the rest of the day's march the commanders clustered about him so closely I could hear and see little. But for a long time he looked dazed and seemed almost inarticulate. Even later, returned to his senses, he was unable to explain what had occurred. He said the same thing over and over. He had seen a cross, he said, a shining cross. Nothing more. But at the day's end he assembled all the leaders of his staff and declared that this was the symbol, and this the god, by which we would conquer. He looked pugilistic, haggard even, but he seemed firmer than in a long time.

Tonight the news is all over the army that the Emperor has become a Christian.

I do not know what more to write. Even what I feel is becoming treason. The Emperor – a Christian. The words dance obscenely together. And they touch me not only with fear, but with bitterness. Constantine – who does not know? – has been racked with pain. But how has he escaped it? By indulging in a lie. Of course the lie, to him, is truth, and he has now clothed himself in the certainty he needs. That is how he will rule. Yes, he has become a god. But less than a man.

This evening I went out into the fields with my servant Cimon, and we stood looking over the hills in the direction of Rome, with heather and cyclamen flowering at our feet. I had the strange impression that this was the last time I would experience such tranquillity, and that very soon everything will be changed. I felt this with a distinctness not to be avoided. Can Constantine turn the Empire Christian? The flowers were bright and the oak trees in the grove of Hercules were quivering in a sharp wind. But nothing touched us. Would these flowers, I wondered, seem the same to eyes which no longer feel as we do, think as we do? No. The mind lends them its own colours. They change to every generation. They are never known. How, I wonder, will these Christians see the world?

But then the world does not much concern the Christians. They are too busy with their own souls. Christianity, I suspect, will be the old age of our civilisation – a time spent repenting the splendours of youth. Perhaps it is fitting that in the failing light of this Empire, once so strong and majestic, we should turn to worship a false promise. The blood has drained out of us and the Christians conquer a ghost.

But what am I most afraid of? Civil war? That Constantine will persecute? That the Germans will conquer us? No. I am afraid that my *Some Aspects of Reason in Epicurus* may never now be published. Such a little thing is man.

XXX

Memoranda of Cecrops.

24 October

TODAY Majesty had the heatstroke bad and falls from horse. He had it renewed times as a boy. But not since. And as a boy he holds the sides of his head. And as a boy he buries his face.

Says he saw cross.

No cross, says I. It was the Sun God struck him.

Give paste of rose oil and powdered quartz.

XXXI

Geta, Master of the Offices, to Tetricus,
Praetorian Prefect.

Confidential   24 October

YOU ask me to send you my written opinion of today's happening. But I imagine it cannot differ substantially from yours.

I did not observe anything unusual in the Augustus' behaviour before his well-simulated vision. He was perhaps preoccupied, and he was perspiring from the sun. As you will recall, I was riding on his left hand at the time. The Marshal declares that His Eternity called out "Fausta", but I did not hear this. I think he merely said "Look! God!", and slid to the ground. In the moment before he leant against his horse I observed that his eyes were not open, as is usual with men who see visions, but were tightly closed.

The Augustus is a practical man. He clearly understands the value which the troops attach to a convincing spiritual experience. And the soldiers, of course, are ecstatic. They say that their Emperor has been personally visited by God and has been granted a sign that he will conquer. They do not care by which god. One god or another, it's much the same to them.

As for the future, the Augustus may well judge Christianity needful for the Empire. I would ask you to consider the following:
1. That although weak in numbers, the Christians form a significant part of the populace. They occupy much of the lower strata of the civil service, and are even to be found among commissioned officers.
2. That due to persecution this has become an admirably organised and resilient religion.
3. That its only comparable rival, the faith of Mithras, has a fatal weakness which goes unnoticed: it is closed to women.
4. Lastly, and most significant, Christianity is the only religion which denies the truth of all the others. Therefore it will not bend. The others will.

The Marshal seems to have been deceived, along with most of the tribunes. They all assume a personal conversion. But it is absurd to separate His Eternity's personal interests from those of the state. He is its guardian and its living symbol.

XXXII

Fausta to Marina.

Narni, 26 October

THE strain has been unbearable here. The townspeople are under curfew and it's quiet as death.

An hour ago an orderly from Gaius' staff arrived with a directive about the passage of provisions. I asked the garrison commander to have him sent to my quarters. The man was intensely excited. When I demanded what was the matter, he prostrated himself before me and said that the Augustus had become a Christian. I thought he must be drunk. But no. The account circulating among the imperial staff is that the Emperor saw a cross shining in the sky above Mount Soracte.

The officers here are incredulous. Ten minutes ago the commander made an excuse to see me, and I've only just got rid of him. Of course he was trying to discover my feelings. But he'd never guess them, my cousin, and nor will you. I feel *jilted*.

The more I think of Gaius' vision the more inevitable it seems. You see, Marina, he has always had this yearning for something absolute. Often with me he appeared like a supplicant seeking to drown himself in worship. He thought it possessiveness, but it was more like a rage for harmony or for death.

Yes, until a little while ago it was in me that he fleshed out this dream of divinity. The flesh rebelled and failed him, of course, but the dream goes on.

The moment I write this I feel ashamed to be reducing the great world of gods and men to my vain self. So female! If you don't understand what I've tried to say, it doesn't matter. At heart I don't understand it myself. And if I did, I couldn't explain it. There are no words for what happens in the mind's dark.

XXXIII

*Hosius, Bishop of Cordoba, to the
Bishop of Ipagrum.*

[Copies of this letter were later circulated to all the dioceses of Nearer Spain.]

27 October

GIVE thanks, beloved in Christ! The king of earth has embraced the King of Heaven!

Not two days ago, while we had crossed the Tiber and were marching into Etruria, a shudder passed through the whole army. The Emperor, it emerged, had been struck from his horse, like Saul on the road to Damascus, and will rise to be a very Paul among us!

Even the Secretary Synesius and the Marshal – a follower of the demon Mithras – speak of it openly. From all accounts the Augustus saw a cross shining in the heavens and burning with the words: 'By this sign conquer!'

As is common in those who have undergone mystic communion, he can scarcely articulate what he experienced. For what is there to say? 'The vision eludes all telling: because how could a man describe the Supreme as detached, when he has seen it as one with himself?' Perhaps, indeed, the Augustus knows less than anybody what has happened. He saw God, and people who see God know nothing. They have no need.

Oh my brother, what wonders the Lord performs! And what a world lies before us!

XXXIV

Tetricus, Praetorian Prefect: taken down verbatim by Synesius.

27 October

. . . By noon we were marching close under Mount Soracte. Many tombs stood on either side of the road, most of them broken or decaying. The Augustus was silent and I thought it odd that he should be sweating. He's fought in the deserts of Persia and Egypt, and he's hard as rock. The legions marched in close order, four abreast. We were all apprehensive. The only buildings in sight were the temple of Apollo on the mountain and the ranks of ruined sepulchres along the road.

Suddenly the Augustus asked me: "Have you heard of the celestial body?"

I'm afraid I laughed, Secretary. I thought he was talking about a woman. Then I looked at him. Even his eyes seemed to be perspiring; they were abnormally bright.

I said: "No."

We moved into the lee of the mountain. He must have been holding his horse on a tight rein, because it kept tossing its head. We passed a deserted post-house and some mausoleums split by tree roots. Their busts and marble inscriptions lay broken about the grass: bits of sentences like 'To the everlasting . . .' or '. . . beloved of so-and-so'. Constantine was breathing hard. All at once he said: "Why is it so dark?" (It wasn't.) He rubbed his eyes, closed them and shook his head, as if ridding his vision of something. For a minute we rode on. I recall that his mouth was pulled back from its teeth, as if the skin was too tight to cover them.

Then he stopped. I think he murmured a question. The Marshal said it was "Fausta?", but I didn't hear it. For a moment he sat stiff in the saddle. His face held the most extraordinary expression. Its very eyes and skin were frozen in terror. He cried "Look!" then "God, god!" not in recognition, but as if he was screaming almost soundlessly for help. The next moment he had slipped over his horse's withers.

You ask for my opinion, Secretary. It is this: I believe that Constantine did not have a vision of light. No. *He had a vision of darkness and chaos.* He saw a universe without order, or God, or any meaning at all.

I knew a man in Gaul who dared not look into the night skies. So he declared the stars did not exist. They were merely dead heroes turned into light, he said, you could touch them with your hand. I suspect that in the same way Constantine, unable to endure what he had seen, spread the Christian cross over that unthinkable abyss.

But who am I to say? I'm a soldier, not a doctor or a priest. The Augustus is now very hard and calm. He no longer wishes to inquire into anything.

And tomorrow we march for Rome.

On October 28th A.D. 312 the rival armies met nine miles north of Rome, and Constantine won an overwhelming victory. The body of Maxentius was recovered from the mud of the Tiber, where he had drowned in flight.

With the accession of Constantine, the Church enjoyed imperial patronage, and paganism slowly fell into disrepute. In 324, when the entire Empire came under his sway, he moved his administration from Rome to Constantinople, where he reigned for another thirteen years.

Bishop Hosius, after a long and distinguished career, died disgraced in 358 at the age of a hundred and two.

The Empress Fausta bore Constantine five children. He put her to death for reasons unknown.

The Emperor himself was not baptised until a few days before he died in May 337. But within his lifetime the cross of his vision triumphed, and Christianity became as it remains today: the pre-eminent religion of the Western world.